The Sneaky HOUSEWIFE

Highly Erotic

GAVIN GRIMEZ

The Un-Orthodox Author

authorHOUSE®

AuthorHouse™
1663 Liberty Drive
Bloomington, IN 47403
www.authorhouse.com
Phone: 1 (800) 839-8640

Published by AuthorHouse 03/05/2018

ISBN: 978-1-5462-3207-0 (sc)
ISBN: 978-1-5462-3206-3 (e)

CHAPTER 1

Introducing: Torri Castle

The Life of a Housewife....... Man-O-Man (takes deep breath) it seems like the work is never done. From washing dirty clothes, to recording My Husbands favorite TV Shows I guess life is just grand (sarcasticly) I say to myself. Every morning I lay in our California King Bed with the smell of my better half's cologne on the pillow next to me. I'm reminded by the sun that shoots through our bedroom blinds, that this will be another boring day full of cooking, cleaning, and catering to the 2-most important men in my life which is My Son "Owen" who is 4-years old, and my beloved work-aloholic Husband "Julius", who works for the Police Department protecting and serving everyone except the needs of his WIFE! Anyway....... As I crawl out of bed at 6:30am as usual with the same routine we been doing for about 5-years now, I smell the aroma of coffee brewing from the kitchen, and the sound of cartoons playing on the television set. Hmmmm...... Thinking to myself while I sit on the toilet stool how nice it would be to hop back in bed and pleasure myself with a "finger quickie" since everybody's occupied with their own personal routine...... Not to mention Julius fell asleep on me lastnight during our movie time which I thought would lead to some passionate love making seeing we haven't had sex in a week (sighs). Oh well, "Up & Att'em" is my motto as I stop daydreaming on the toilet, unraveling the tissue to wipe my throbbing pussy from not just the urine, but the juices that I acquired from my thighs being warmly closed overnight sleeping. As soon as I'm in eye view of my son, he quickly stops watching TV and runs toward me with the brightest eyes and the most innocent look a kid could enhance; "mommy mommy mommy" he yields as we hug each other like we haven't seen each other in decades. "Good morning Owen" I replied back "Mommy missed you baby"! I glanced over towards the breakfast table and see Julius reading his morning newspaper (sports section) and sipping on the coffee I smelled earlier while laying horny in our satin sheeted bed. "Goodmorning My King" I said to Julius, who seemed to be only interested in the game scores from lastnight. "Goodmorning My Queen" he spoke back, and instantly my face lit up like the 4th of July yearning for that morning kiss from his lips to mine before he goes to work for 10-hours of torture. As we kiss I whisper in his ear, hoping Owen is paying more attention to his cartoons and not his horn-ball of a Mother, gently in Julius's ear I say "How about you skip work today baby, and focus on handcuffing, strip-searching, and detaining your Wife in our bedroom all day today"!!! He then gives me a look as if he's interested in my proposal but just needs a little more convincing. I then yell in the other room to Owen telling him "Don't forget your book bag Son"….. hoping it's in his bedroom so I can have more alone time with Julius to convince him to stay home and fuck me. As Owen gets up from watching TV to go find this mysterious book bag, I quickly grab Julius's hand and let him feel my panty-less phat ass under my silk gown that he's been neglecting for a week now. I feel his strong masculine hand slide his fingers down the crack of my ass, searching for the moisture between my legs, hoping that the wetness will arouse him and I'll get the pussy pounding I deserve after 7-days of a sex-less marriage. His finger tips finally found my purring pussycat, and after watching his pants rise in the front of his zipper I'm guessing he's pleased with my juice box so far. As he sticks one finger inside, I confess how good it makes me feel and how much I want the real thing instead, then he sticks two fingers inside my thirsty vagina and my mouth just waters for more not even being able to speak, but a definite moan finds its way out of my mouth. Gripping the counters in the kitchen with my hands, I damn near broke my freshly manicured nails from the pleasure of my husband and his magical hand trick he must of recently possessed overnight. One by one he pulls his fingers out of my fuzzy faucet, and I watch him lick the white creamy residue off his hands so seductively I start biting my bottom lip just watching. With no time to waste, Julius spins me around arching my back with the intent that I've been a very bad girl, and that there's a spanking coming soon cause of my naughtiness. Facing the opposite way of my (Morning Lover) I can't see what's to come next, but the thrill of not knowing is starting to become better than sex itself, and I can't explain the feeling. Then I feel his tongue on my ankles sliding wetly up to my calf, and then tongue kissing the back of my knee. With both hands on my milky B-cup breast, I feel tickles of a slow pace mouth heading between my ass cheeks with tiny nibbles & bites each time his nose goes in my asshole. The feeling of Julius licking my clit from the back, all the way up to my asshole makes me want to cry and smile at the same damn time. As his tongue climbs up to my ear lobe, I'm ready to give him my mind, body, and soul no matter the price. He whispers in my ear while playing with my nipples.... "How bad do you want this dick"? I replied "I want that dick so bad baby, I'll get on my knees right now in this kitchen and worship your cock like it was Jesus Christ himself"! I heard his pants unbuckle, and next thing I know I was being slammed on our kitchen counter-top face down with my thick juicy ass in the air for the taking. I felt his dick creeping at the bottom of my ass cheeks, thinking to myself....(Thank God I didn't masturbate earlier cause my small little finger definitely can't compare to my husband's 9-inch love muscle), and I didn't want to waste another orgasm on pleasuring myself but instead; proving my loyalty to Julius by Niagara Falling all over his manhood. He then slides that rock hard dick inside me gently pulling my hair at the same time whispering.... "Is this what My Queen wants"? I respond back....."[Yes My King this is exact]" and before I could finish my sentence I hear.... "mommy mommy I found my book bag"! Owen confused says "Why is daddy whispering in your ear so close"? "That's not nice mommy, you said we don't keep secrets in this house or whisper about each other"! I responded as quickly as I could while breathing excessively cause Julius's penis pounder was still very much inside of me. "No honey, we're not keeping secrets, Daddy was just giving me a kiss before he leaves to take you to school, now don't you come in this kitchen without washing your hands in the bathroom ok"! As soon as Owen leaves our vicinity we fix ourselves back to the presentable parents we portray to be in everyday life. Those three penetrated strokes I received from Julius before we were childly interrupted was awesome but not full-filling, seeing that this would be Day #8 I haven't had my just due. Julius quickly gives me a goodbye kiss, then Owen gave me a goodbye hug & kiss, and in a instant their gone for the day and I'm in a empty house. Meanwhile….. my silk gown keeps finding its way between my ass crack sticking to me every chance it gets courtesy of the water show initiated by my unfinished business of a husband. Just when I thought my masturbation days were coming to an end, looks like me and my finger are back in a relationship once again (sighs) This definitely gives a new meaning to the middle finger saying (FUCK YOU)!!

CHAPTER 2

Introducing Julius Castle

Beep Beep Beep! Goes the alarm clock I set for 6:00am every morning for my demanding job as a Police Officer. As I lay in bed before getting up to shower and wake up my son for another school day, I can't help but notice how much of a routine these last 5-years have been for me and my wife. Watching her sleep next to me gives me peace, and assures me that love really does conquer all, especially after seeing all the hatred that these streets have to offer while I'm at work. Hopefully Torri's not mad at me from last night cause I did fall asleep on our movie that we we're watching. I'm thinking I should rollover and please her with my mouth & dick this morning, but she's sleeping so peaceful I think I'll just hop in the shower and wake Owen up for school. Feeling so fresh and clean I turn the television on for my son and make a pot of coffee so I can start this 10-hour shift of torture. As my wife wakes up and makes her way in the kitchen, I watch the connection her and my son share, and it makes me feel like the luckiest man alive. If she could only read my mind as I look at her with that silk gown on, knowing that she's naked as fuck under all of that, the things I would do if Owen wasn't in the other room watching cartoons. Well....... like I mentioned before, me and Owen kiss our favorite lady goodbye, and off to work I proceed as usual; this same damn routine. The smell of doughnuts & coffee when I walk in the precinct still does something to me after 10-years on the force, and I must admit I look forward to it, as if it brings some kind of safety to my soul. Stacks of reports and paperwork invade my desk so there's definitely not a dull moment as a cop in this city. Even though my work load is heavy, I still can't get that image out of my head of that little boy and man I killed three months ago. The little boy jumped in front of gunfire trying to protect a man whom we believe is owner of the house. The bullet pierced through the boy's chest and still managed to kill the man behind him as well. The man attempted to pull a weapon which we later discovered was an "Air Pellet Rifle". Bullets or pellets don't matter, because at that precise moment when you're a cop, all we see is the rifle, so of course we assumed that it was a real shotgun. Truthfully the man's death didn't bother me to much, but that kid reminds me of my son, and it got me thinking real hard about Owen's safety out here in these streets. My Captain is making me see a therapist just in case I have anything I need to get off my chest, but really needs to know if I'm capable of carrying my weapon on the job without any regret or hesitation in the future. A woman named Dr. Robinson called my captain offering her services to the department, and he quickly recommended her to me. Our first therapy session was a success, but honestly I couldn't keep my eyes off her beauty. She was about 5'5 in height, semi long hair style that put you in the mind of a famous celebrity, tits were about C or D cups, and an ass to die for. She was wearing a semi-short business suit skirt with the thigh high stockings, and every time she crossed her legs I damn near spilled my coffee all over myself. I immediately told her about my beautiful family that I had at home, basically trying to jinx myself so I could think of my wife and not of her sexy ass. After showing her pictures of my wife & son she replied…. "You have a beautiful family, and you're a very lucky man Mr. Castle, family is so important now a days. Make sure you look after them closely because they could be taken away at the blink of an eye in this cold world we live in"! I nodded my head in agreement, and replied…. "You're absolutely correct Miss Robinson"!! After leaving her office I felt relieved & refreshed even though we didn't discuss much, it still felt good being in her presence and having someone listen to me with her beauty. Walking in the house after another hard day's work was normal……The smell of fried chicken roamed the house, Owen drawing silly pictures at the kitchen table while Torri cooked, and the radio playing Oldies but Goodies just like we liked. I walked over to my wife as she sweated over the stove wearing one of my t-shirts, and a pair of Leggings that showed off her physique to perfection. "Hey Bay what you over here cooking" as I grabbed her waist and kissed her neck. She replied….." Just a little something something sweetie"! Her neck smelled so good, you can tell she just got out the shower waiting on Big Daddy to get home. I informed her that I just had my first therapy session with a Dr. Robinson at work today, and she's going to help me get through this rough patch I'm going through about that little boy from three months ago. Torri was glad I was getting a little extra help after dealing with that horrific incident that basically my job requires. The way she looked at the situation is..... If I didn't shoot first I probably would be dead, and her and Owen would be making funeral arrangements for me instead of the other way around. After greeting my family upon my arrival, I rubbed Owen's head while he drew his pictures, and then made my way to the bedroom so I could shower, change clothes, and then get ready for dinner. In the bedroom I noticed Torri had an outfit laid out on the bed that consisted of a nice tight shirt to show off those B-cup tits of hers, and a short mini skirt that I couldn't wait to see her in. I assume she's just picking out possible outfits to wear for our (Date Night) tomorrow that we have every weekend for the last year or so since we acquired a babysitter. I clean up nicely and then mosey my way back to the kitchen so I can eat dinner. The food looks delicious, and after 10-hours on the job I'm hungrier than a damn hostage. While eating I mentioned to Torri that I definitely approved of the mini skirt that was laid on our bed, and couldn't wait to see that plump ass in it tomorrow night. Little does she know, I have a big surprise for my bored housewife on our special (Date Night)!

CHAPTER 3

DATE NIGHT

TORRI:

Thank god for Friday's & Saturday nights when you're a housewife. No cooking in a hot ass house, I order pizza & wings for Owen, and Me and Julius go out for dinner and a movie like clockwork every weekend. We hired a babysitter about a couple months ago to watch our son, hoping we can rekindle that fire we once had a long time ago when we first met. The babysitter name is Amanda, she's about 22-years old, new college student, big breast that she flaunts around like nobody's business, and secretly has a crush on my husband, but I'm not supposed to notice I guess. Anyway......while picking through my closet I'm trying to find the perfect outfit to make Julius drool over me all night while we're out and about. In the process of me finding the right heels to wear with my short mini skirt, here comes this little bitch [I mean Amanda]; in my room including her two cents toward my wardrobe.

AMANDA:

I was thinking Mrs. Castle you should wear these boots with that instead of heels. I really think Mr. Castle would like to see you in those instead.

TORRI:

In my head I'm thinking… "Bitch, how would you know what my husband wants to see me in with your young ass"!! But the only thing that actually came out my mouth was…. Why thank you Amanda, I'll ask Julius when he gets home, by the way where is Owen you're supposed to be watching him while I get dressed.

AMANDA:

He's in the other room watching TV waiting on the pizza man to get here. Matter of fact let me go check on him, because he is being a little too quiet in there for a 4-year old.

TORRI:

Ok, you go do that and I'll finish getting dressed [Lil Bitch] I whisper under my breath with the look like I'm tired of your ass.

JULIUS:

(Honey I'm Home)! I'm yelling throughout the entire house. Owen dives in my arms as if he didn't already see me this morning. I speak to Amanda while I take off my jacket. I'm starting to suspect that our babysitter has a little crush on me, cause she does a lot of dry flirting from time to time, and she loves hugging me with those big ass tits she possess. If Owen was a little older, I think he would appreciate the babysitter his old man hired to watch over him LOL.

TORRI:

Hey babe….. I need your opinion on which shoes to wear with this mini skirt. Should I wear these heels or these boots? He immediately picked the boots just like Amanda assured me he would.

AMANDA:

I told u Mrs. Castle, men love women in boots while wearing a skirt

TORRI:

You sure did Amanda, (I said out loud) but in my head I was thinking.... "Julius definitely going to have to fire this cunt, and even though he's not aware that he chose her side about that whole shoe/boot ordeal, he isn't getting no pussy tonight either!! [Fuck Everybody] OK OK......Let me stop being such a bitch. This is me and my husband's night on the town, and I'm not gone let this young little broad ruin my joy, especially since I been waiting on this damn weekend all week. As me and Julius were leaving out the door we both gave Owen a hug & kiss and told Amanda we would be back home at a reasonable time, and that she should call us if any type of emergency was to occur. Julius opened my car door like the gentlemen I knew he was, and for a minute I start feeling like a young girl again on her way to Homecoming or Prom with the love of my life. While driving I noticed that Julius passed our favorite restaurant that we go to every weekend. I said....." Babe you just passed the restaurant where are we going"?

JULIUS:

I know baby, I wanted to be spontaneous and take you somewhere different since it seems like we always do the same stuff every weekend. [winks eye]

TORRI:

Oh My God baby, it feels like you just read my mind. I didn't want to say anything because I know you work so hard, and I know how Police Officers try to stick to certain places to eat, shop, etc..... cause of safety precautions. But if you don't mind me asking..... "Where is this New Place" we're going too"?

JULIUS:

It's a surprise, but I'll give you a hint....... It's a lot of Live Entertainment for us to enjoy while we eat & drink. But since we're on the topic, why didn't you tell me that you were bored of the same routine honey? I'm so distracted by my job, I never really noticed if you're enjoying yourself in this marriage or just content with the usual. How about starting today, we stop holding things back, speak what's on our minds, and we do everything in our power to make sure we have another 5-years of eternal bliss.

TORRI:

Sounds like a perfect plan to me baby, I feel like a huge load just got took off my shoulder at this moment. I then glanced out the window and noticed us slowing down to a crowded parking lot with bright lights, and a woman statue on top of the building. I look over at Julius and say.... "No yo ass didn't bring me to a Strip Club"! (with a tiny smurk on my face)

JULIUS:

You damn right I did!! Today is a new day for us Torri, we gone broaden our horizons and I'm going to pay for your first lap dance as a married woman. (slight giggle)

TORRI:

You definitely are full of all kind of surprises tonight huh? As the valet driver takes our car away, my heart is beating tremendously as I grab my hubby's hand and we walk inside this Pussy Palace of naked women and bundles of alcohol, we finally found a nice booth not too far from the bar, but a little ways away from the performing stage. I asked Julius screaming over the loud music.... "Is this your first time coming here, or are you a regular"?

JULIUS:

Honestly, I drove pass here a million times telling myself to stop in and have a beer, but I never seem to have the time too. I actually made these plans for us to come here tonight about a week ago. I wanted to share this experience with you and only you sweetheart. Call me old-fashioned but I'm actually in love with my wife (kiss kiss)!

TORRI:

After that kiss, it felt like it was just Me and Him in that club by ourselves. My brain cut out all the loud music, and for a second I didn't even notice the thirsty men or naked women that surrounded us in the bar.

JULIUS:

Excuse me..... Waitress! I would like to order a couple drinks for me and my wife we're first timers. She replied... "Go ahead with your order Sir". Okay, let me have (4-shots of tequila/ a sex on the beach/ and whatever imported beer you have available it doesn't really matter. Oh..... and send over your prettiest girl for a lap dance to our booth. Thank You!

TORRI:

I never been so nervous in my life. The anticipation of this woman on her way over to our booth half naked was over-whelming. Julius seemed calm & collected while waiting on her to come over, and then I look up and there she was......smooth skin with glitter covering her body, pink matching bra & thong set, and the sexiest legs I ever seen on a woman.

JULIUS:

Nice to meet you. My name is Julius, and this is my wife Torri. She immediately assumes that the lap dance is for me, but I quickly re-direct her to make better acquaintance with my wife while she looks confused. I tell her…. "This is my wife's first time inside a Strip Club, and this will be her first lap dance as well". She grabs my wife hand, and gently pulls her out of her seat and proceeds to the VIP Room. I wave at both of them with my drink in hand, and yell…. "You two be good now"!!

TORRI:

I can't believe this is happening to me, I tell myself that I'm a married woman and have no business going in this VIP Room with this strange woman that I don't even know. Every chance I get to turn around, and say no no no I changed my mind, my feet won't seem to stop walking forward with this glittered lady. As we play follow the leader, we get to this so called (VIP Room) and it definitely was built for discretion. She sits me down on the couch, and proceeds to tease & tantalize me with her sweaty tits and oily ass. At that exact moment something inside my body started tingling with the weirdess feeling. Her body was amazing, and I could actually smell her pussy with a mixture of body lotion and body spray combined. What is going on? (I'm thinking to myself) all this time I thought only Julius could make me feel this way, especially how I'm feeling between my legs right now. She got closer and we made eye contact as if she was a man and I was her woman for the night. Then she grabbed my hand and placed it on her soft breast while her hand found its way on mine. Every part of me wanted her and I couldn't believe she had me open like this after only 2-3 minutes in this VIP Room. Her hand slid up my mini skirt so passionately, right around my panties, heading straight for my creamy interior. I could have stopped her, but honestly I didn't want too. I followed suit just as she did, and found myself sticking my finger inside of her wet pussy as well. Once I pulled my finger out of her, I couldn't believe how intoxicating the smell of a woman was, and now things was starting to make sense of why men love eating, tasting, and licking pussy!! She smiled while I was caught up in ecstasy and offered to feed it to me if I was up to the challenge. I then laid her down on the couch that I was sitting on, and start kissing her nipples one by one. After so long, kissing wasn't enough and my body yearned for licking & sucking! I sucked her tits like they were my husband's dick with the pressure of my pussy ready

13

to bust through my panties. My tongue slid down to her belly button like it had a mind of its own, and the aroma of her kitty kat was just begging to get eaten up. I swear I had no idea what I was doing down there, cause usually I'm the one laying down with a head between my legs on a regular day. As my tongue goes to work like never before on this Exotic Goddess, I found myself hornier then I ever been in my life which was confusing because I love my husband, but my husband doesn't have a pussy either. Then the craziest thing happened after so many licks I presented across her raging clitoris. A gush of juices flowed out of her pussy while she moaned and gripped my head to stay down there and finish my task. (Oh My God)........ I yelled!! Thinking she just urinated in my mouth, but she quickly explained that she was a squirter.... and for me to be a first timer, I definitely was a keeper. You would think after all that erotic behavior we just displayed in this secret room, we were in there for hours, but NO! It only took 15-minutes for me to find out that my new found pleasure was women this whole time. The exotic goddess gave me a napkin to wipe all those love juices off my face, and a seductive kiss, then sent me on my way. My brain was moving in a hundred different places as I walked back to the booth where my husband was waiting patiently for his newly improved wife. I approached Julius with the most dangerous kiss hoping he wouldn't smell the wettest pussy I ever tasted still lingering on my lips. He kissed me back and said......

JULIUS:

So how was it babe? You were in there for a nice little minute, did you enjoy your first lap dance experience?

TORRI:

Yes I did, and now I'm ready to go. I want take you home right now and make sweet love to you like never before. I confessed to him that me and my new found friend just did the nastiest things you could imagine in that VIP Room, and I hope you're not disappointed in me.

JULIUS:

Oh really?!?! Well listen baby.... the VIP Room only cost $20, and I gave her $100 so she could show you the time of your life. My love for you just got deeper than ever Torri, because you could have returned back to me and lied by saying nothing happen in there but a innocent lap dance, but you didn't. You told me the truth about everything, and that my dear is the biggest turn-on a husband could endure. Oh yeah, by the way......I can still smell her all over your face [Laugh] I'm glad you had fun though sweetie.

TORRI:

After all the wiping I did to my pretty face, messing up my make-up and smearing my lip gloss; he still noticed that intoxicating smell from her purging vagina all over me. As we drove back home our love connection seemed to be the freshest it's ever been in 5-years of marriage. I couldn't keep my eyes off of his pants, just imagining his dick under his boxers just waiting to be sucked at the next red light we approached. I couldn't refrain as I unzipped his pants and grabbed his penis to insert it in my mouth. Knowingly we were only a couple blocks away from home, and I actually could have just waited, but I had to have him at that exact moment no questions asked. As I sucked & spit all over him, his head just rocked back and forth with the pleasure of a horny housewife at his service. I then stopped as we approached the house wiping that dick off my breath with a faint scent of pussy still on there as well from the secret room. I asked him while we sat in the driveway outside our house.... "Do you think Amanda likes you"? I noticed that she stares at you a lot, and always seem to have the skimpiest shirts on when she comes over to watch Owen every weekend.

JULIUS:

Yea I have noticed, but I pay her no mind because I already have you My Queen. I did over hear her on the phone one day talking to someone about a sexual encounter she must have had with a woman recently. It was really none of my business, but you know…. me being a cop, I definitely had to get my ease-dropping on [Laughing]

TORRI:

Oh my…. Amanda likes women? I swear I didn't know that, but who am I too judge (shit) I didn't know I liked women myself until tonight [laugh]

JULIUS:

I tell you what Torri. How would you like to have sex with Me and another woman one of these days strictly confidential? I'm starting to notice that you really enjoy pussy, and I know how much you like my dick as well…. So maybe you should try both!

TORRI:

That would definitely be a New Experience for me babe, but I just want to assure you that…. "I'm Not Attracted "Too Any Other Men Except You", And I Swear That This Pussy Has Your Name Written All Over It Boo"!! Please don't look at me in a different way because I like women, and you have to promise Julius that you will never throw this in my face or mention this to anyone else, me being a housewife and all I really want to keep this behind closed doors ok sweetie!

JULIUS:

Don't worry honey, your pussy….. I mean your secret is safe with me [giggles]! Hey……. I got a crazy idea once we walk in the house. Since we both think Amanda has a crush on me, maybe she could be our first threesome since we know she likes men & women. When we walk in, you go straight to the bedroom and I'll go pay Amanda, while you're checking on Owen I'll see if she's interested in some playtime with us.

TORRI:

Ok, but what if she says NO?

JULIUS:

Then I'll blame it on the alcohol and she can take her ass home! It's just that simple.

TORRI:

As we walk in the house, we see Amanda laying on the couch under a sheet acting nervous trying her best to turn off the TV so we can't see what she was watching.

AMANDA:

Hey you guys! I didn't know you two were coming back so early. I wasn't doing anything..... just watching a movie [studdering voice]

TORRI:

What were you watching? And why are you naked under the sheet?

AMANDA:

Hmmmm I was watching...... Ok guys I can't lie, I was watching a porno but I swear I didn't know you would be home so soon. Please don't fire me, I really need this job to help me pay for school.

JULIUS:

We're not mad at you Amanda. We out of all people know the needs that people want sexually, as a matter of fact cut the TV back on so we can see what you were enjoying before we interrupted you.

TORRI:

Yes Amanda, were not mad at all. Let me go check on Owen, and then we can all watch it together when I get back.

AMANDA:

Are you sure guys? I really feel uncomfortable laying here on your couch naked watching porn. How about I just watched Owen for free tonight, and we keep this little secret between us.

JULIUS:

No problem Amanda, we definitely know how to keep a secret especially after the night we just had!

TORRI:

I walked back in the front room after checking on Owen who was sleeping like an Angel in his bed. I approached Julius & Amanda on the couch in the living room while the porn was playing in the background. I slowly pull the sheet from off of Amanda and see those big juicy breast with the hardest nipples begging to be sucked. She looked at me with a confused look on her face and said.....

AMANDA:

Mrs. Castle what are you doing? I didn't know you were interested in women. Well….. since your staring so hard at my tits, why don't you taste one while you're at it.

JULIUS:

Yeah babe…. let me see you pretty ladies please each other while I watch, and if you're interested I can go get my handcuffs to make things more interesting.

TORRI:

Her tits were so big I couldn't even get my mouth around them, but once I licked the nipple she started going crazy. Her craziness made me so wet my mini skirt just rose up by itself. Amanda's hand was up my skirt, and it started feeling like a sequel to the strip club we just left a hour ago. I laid back on the couch and let her tongue just bathe between my legs. I was turned on by her eating my pussy, but I was more turned on knowing Julius was sitting across from us just watching like a eagle scouting his prey. His dick was standing taller than the Eifel Tower, and watching him stroke it up & down just made me even more anxious. He walked over, dick in hand and just stuck it in my mouth with no hesitation. Pussy being ate while sucking my hubby's dick at the same time felt like heaven. Julius then pulled his cock out of my mouth…. grabbed Amanda by her hair, and then stuck his throbbing penis inside her mouth while making me watch. Seeing him get head from another woman made me so fucking hot, I started playing with my pussy so fast….. rubbing and sticking my finger inside myself, pinching my nipples, and even start licking his balls while Amanda serviced the dick that I've enjoyed for 5-years. He then bent me over the couch and finally gave me all that dick that I deserved, and been anticipating for 8 going on 9 days now. As soon as it went inside me, my eyes rolled in the back of my head and I start remembering why I married this generous love machine of a man. Amanda definitely wasn't an amateur or new to this situation I noticed. She positioned herself under me in the 69 position on the couch while Julius was fucking my brains out from the back. While that stiff dick went in & out of me, she was licking my clit at the same time, and just when I thought those two things was just what I needed….. Julius slid a finger in my asshole and I swear to god I just went bananas. Trying my hardest not to explode because I was enjoying every second of this threesome, I couldn't take anymore. My orgasm soaked poor little Amanda's face and chest, and drenched hubby's cock all over everywhere. Amanda jumped up trying to breathe catching any piece of oxygen she could find that god provided for us on this earth. Not trying to be funny or anything like that, but all I could think of was what the girl in the VIP Room told me earlier after this similar incident which was; "I didn't urinate in your mouth Amanda, I'm a squirter! And for this to be your first threesome, your definitely a keeper"!! (I giggled on the inside)

JULIUS:

WHOA!!! Damn honey, you never squirted before, where did that come from?

TORRI:

I told you I was backed up for a week Bae, I guess you were just hitting the right spots. (But I knew the real reason of that water show was my new lust for pussy, but I couldn't tell Julius that)

AMANDA:

Jesus Mrs. Castle!! I already took a shower today, but thanks for the extra bath [Laugh] and by the way….. This isn't my first threesome either (winks eye)

TORRI:

Julius then stuck his shaft back in my dripping cunt gripping my waist with each thrust while Amanda sat watching.... playing with her tight shaved little pussy. He exploded inside of me digging his finger tips into my love handles, and I accepted every drip. Thank god I'm on birth control or Owen definitely would have had a brother or sister prior to tonight's action packed events.

CHAPTER 4

THE GARDEN COMPETITION

Every year in July our neighborhood has an Annual "Flower Garden Competition", and every year Mr. & Mrs. Baxter win's with flying colors. With little credit too myself I actually came in 2nd Place last year, and Julius was so proud. The Baxter's are about 60-years old, and with the time they have on their hands, I'm not surprised that there not victorious every year. After me and my husband's date night at the strip club, and our little encounter with the babysitter, I suddenly have a streak of confidence and refuse to lose this year's Garden Challenge! I only have 1-week to get my yard into shape so off to Home Depot I go. Once inside the store I found everything I needed plus extras to make my garden the best on the block. At the register I couldn't believe my eyes….. "$250.00" for everything I had in my basket….. Oh man, Julius is going to kill me once the bank statement comes in the mail. Then I remembered (Duh) I'm the one who gets all the mail that comes too our house anyway, so I'll just intercept that envelop and nobody will ever know. Honestly I don't give a fuck if the total came up to "$500.00" dollars, whatever it takes for me to beat those old ass Baxter's I'm going to do it. So finally I get home, and I start unloading all the materials I need to be #1. Across the street I see Mrs. Baxter working in her garden preparing for the competition I assume. We wave at each other just like neighbors suppose too, but we never liked each other ever since we moved in this house. A couple days go by and I must admit, I've got our yard looking immaculate! And it better be after spending "$250.00" dollars at home depot the other day. But for some reason, those damn Baxter's yard still looked better than mine and I can't understand it. As I go check our mail for the day, I don't know if it was fate, destiny, or whatever you want to call it, but some of the Baxter's mail ended up in my mailbox. Being the 2nd Place bitch that I am, I should tear they motherfucking mail up and throw it away, but I figured I'm a good sport, so I'll deliver it to them personally. A couple houses down I spotted the Mail Truck which was kind of strange, cause he's usually never in our neighborhood at this time…. not to mention me being a bored ass housewife, these are things you tend to know when you're at home all damn day. I changed my mind about going to the Baxter's and figured I'll just take it down to the mail truck instead, that way I don't have to see Mrs. Baxter's wrinkled ass face, and I can get a little extra exercise since I haven't been to the gym in like a month. On my way down to the truck, the Baxter's loud ass television caught my ear, and I sort of changed my mind again about dropping this piece of mail off personally. I approach their doorbell and noticed that the door was kind of cracked open….. so I spoke loudly; "Hello Mrs. Baxter, I had some of your mail in my box so I decided to bring it over"! I guess the TV was so loud nobody could hear me. I crept in the house slowly heading straight to where the loud TV was, but there was nobody there. I then heard a noise coming from upstairs and thought….. I know there old so their probably deaf as well, but I didn't turn off the TV. I made my way up the stairs and as I got closer I started hearing slight moaning with other pieces of mail on some of the steps. Oh My God I thought to myself! This sneaky old bitch is fucking the mailman!! Then I start thinking this is just what I needed to win the Garden Competition……. I catch Mrs. Baxter with the mailman, blackmail her ass, and I win 1st Place, oh wow Julius & Owen will be so proud of me. More moans come from the bedroom so I have to think quickly….. Damn I left my cellphone at home, so how am I going to record or even take a picture for this blackmail idea to even work? Fuck it…. I could go run home and get it real fast, but being the nosey housewife that I am, my feet won't let me move off these steps. I just have to see what's going on in that room first, than I'll shoot over to the house and grab my phone. Finally approaching the top stair I can see the mailman with his head to the sky receiving the best blow job he probably ever received while on the clock. Then I get a little closer and see Mrs. Baxter wearing the ugliest wig I ever seen in my life. (Like I said before)….. Me and her really don't like each other that much, so I'm always looking for things or ways to talk shit about her, but I never seen her wear that hideous wig before. Now I figure this would be the perfect time to run home and get my phone…. because not only is she cheating on her husband, but she's looking ugly while she's doing it, and this right up my alley [laugh]. But me being sneaky little Torri, I had to stick around for more action. At this point I just can't get enough, but something just didn't seem right as I got closer to the bedroom door. The mailman's hand was on top of Mrs. Baxter's head moving that ugly ass wig around until (slip slip) the wig came off! Wait a minute….. that isn't Mrs. Baxter's head underneath that pile of disaster…… (Holy Shit) I just witnessed Mr. Baxter sucking the mailman's dick, I quickly put my hands over my mouth with disgust. I peek in again because I just can't believe it, and for the second time my eyes witnessed the same thing again. He was actually doing a better job than most females I've seen on the pornos. Shiiiiiid he was doing better job than me when I please Julius. (Ok ok ok, what the next move Torri?) Should I still go home and get the cellphone, I mean…… One Baxter is just as good as the next one right? [I say to myself] Fuck it, I fly down the stairs out of the Baxter's home, I run across their yard trying my best to fuck up every flower they ever planted on the way to my house. I busted through my door searching for my phone and finally find it. Back out my house, rushing back over to the Baxter's hoping their nasty asses is still making whoopie. I find myself back on those undelivered mailed stairs quiet as a mouse with cellphone in hand ready to record the most disturbing shit I ever seen in my life. I approach the bedroom and things are even worst then the last time, I almost threw up in my mouth. The mailman had Mr. Baxter bent over on the bed wigless and very un-tasteful. I got all the footage I needed, and couldn't wait to get home and prepare for my 1st Place victory later on this week. As I scimmed through the pictures & video I damn near threw up on myself. I want to show Julius so bad when he gets off work, so we can be disgusted together, but if I do that he'll know I cheated to win the competition, and I can't let him know that. Another thing I thought about was….. (If I do win the competition, Julius won't be mad about the "$250.00" dollars I spent out of our joint bank account because he'll be so proud of his wife). Two days left until the competition and I'm feeling confident as fuck. My garden was looking presentable to the public, and my secret weapon was in my phone just waiting to blackmail Mr. Baxter's nasty ass. I head back to home depot to pick up a few more minor things for my yard, and once inside the store guess who I seen in Aisle #9? That's right you guessed it…. "Mr. Baxter"!! I wasn't even going down Aisle #9 but after I seen his gay ass I couldn't help myself. Sarcasticly I speak……" How you doing MR. B A X T E R" (dragging my words)!

MR. BAXTER:

Hey how you doing Torri, where's that no good husband of yours? I know he's not making you shop for heavy equipment all by yourself.

TORRI:

No no….. I'm just here picking up a few things for the Annual Garden Competiton. [Thinking to myself "Gay ass looking for my husband, probably want to suck him off in Aisle 69, oh well sorry that's my dick faggot"]!!!

MR. BAXTER:

Yea Torri, same thing I'm here doing here. By the way, while you were home yesterday did you see anyone in our front yard? Our flowers and grass were demolished! Looked like somebody just ran through our yard destroying every flower we planted for the competition.

TORRI:

As a matter of fact I did see someone in your yard yesterday, but weren't you guys home? I heard your television set blasting all the way outside.

MR. BAXTER:

Well no….. Me and Mrs. Baxter was at the hospital yesterday. She's having surgery tomorrow, but the doctor said she should be in good health by the time the garden competition takes place.

TORRI:

Listen Up Fuck Stick!! Don't play coy with me alright, your little secret is out ok, and I have the evidence to prove it!

MR. BAXTER:

Excuse me….. Did you just call me "Fuck Stick"??

TORRI:

You damn right I did! I know exactly who was in your yard yesterday (ME)!! I can't believe your trying to play stupid, and even though I really don't like your wife, I feel bad for her that she has a down low ass husband who is 60-years old, and probably wasted half her life with your disgusting ass. Not to mention she's about to have surgery (sighs) You should be ashamed of yourself. But you know what….. I'm done talking I'll just let you see yourself on this "Home Movie" I recorded yesterday. Here it is right in my phone "Take A Look"……

MR. BAXTER:

LMFAO!! You sneaky little bitch, what the hell were you doing in my house? Your husband is a Police Officer, so you out of all people should know that is Breaking & Entering!

TORRI:

Sorry Sir….. but like I told you earlier your TV was blasting, and the door was cracked open. Maybe next time you'll tell your mail order boyfriend to lock the door once he comes inside your house. Or, were you to horny and forgot to lock it, while your pour old wife lay's helplessly in the hospital.

MR. BAXTER:

I guess you're just the little detective huh? Taking pointers from your husband Julius I see. I admit it though, these pictures & video you have in your phone is very disturbing, and I would hate for them to get out.

TORRI:

Exactly, so what you're going to do is….. Drop out of this year's garden competition and I won't expose your little freaky escapades with our mailman. Once I've won the competition I'll delete everything in front of you, and nobody has to know about your little secret.

MR. BAXTER:

That's what this is about…. "The Garden Competition"? (LMAO) I really hate to do this, because I'm actually learning so much about you today that I didn't know in the last 5-years we been neighbors but, look at the video again Mrs. Castle do you see the tattoo on the mailman's hand?

TORRI:

Yeah, so what! I watched this abomination a hundred times, what's your point?

MR. BAXTER:

Oh…. Well let me inform you then Miss Smart Ass, that tattoo is an army tattoo. Now look at the arm on your video of the person sucking the mailman's dick….. (Same tattoo right)?

TORRI:

Stop with the mind games ok, what's the fucking point!

MR. BAXTER:

Pull my sleeve up……Oh my god what do you know, for some reason I don't have that tattoo on my arm on my arm. But how could I had a tattoo yesterday, and it's gone today? Not to mention I was never in the army either!! [Laughs]

TORRI:

What the fuck??

MR. BAXTER:

That's my "Twin Brother" Miss Detective [giggles]…. He lives across town, and was House-sitting for us while Me & my wife were at the hospital yesterday. And that nasty ass mailman you like to disrespect is his husband. They met in the army, and were dishonorably discharged for being homosexuals. As the young generation would say….. "Now you can pick your face up"!! And it's a good thing you're here at home depot too, cause now you can buy all the materials you need to fix "My Yard" that you admitted destroying. I definitely will be telling your husband about this conversation also……(Sneaky Little Bitch)!! Have a nice day detective.

TORRI:

Awwww shit….. Julius is gone kill me! I already spent "$250.00" on our yard, and now I have to replace the Baxter's yard as well. I felt so stupid just standing in that Aisle at home depot, I was still stuck in amazement that Mr. Baxter had a fucking twin……I mean, what was the chances of some shit like that happening. Well let me get home and cook dinner, still have to pick Owen up from Daycare, and Julius will be home in a couple hours. I guess it's time to face the music (sigh). Anyother day it seems as if Julius takes forever to get home, but today he came home at the speed of light. Feeling like a kid that got in trouble at school waiting on the teacher to call the house, I held our cordless phone with the tightest grip waiting on Mr. Baxter to call my husband but he never did. With the same methods of a stalker I watched the Baxter's house through the window while I cooked, but the car wasn't in their driveway.

JULIUS:

The yard is looking amazing honey, I think you're a shoe in to win 1st Place this year at the Garden Competition.

TORRI:

Why thank you sweetie, I worked really hard on it, but for some reason I think the Baxter's are going to win again this year (with guilt in my voice). By the way hun…. "Did you know Mr. Baxter had a twin brother"?

JULIUS:

Yeah I did, but did you know he was gay as well?

TORRI:

Oh no babe, I didn't know that. Hoping he didn't notice in my face that I've been a bad misbehaving wife trying to blackmail elderly people for a damn contest.

JULIUS:

Yep, he's definitely representing the rainbow. As a matter of fact, he's married to our mailman. I guess they met in the army or whatever. Mr. Baxter introduced me to him and his husband last year at the garden competition when they won 1st Place, I thought you knew all this time.

TORRI:

Nope, I guess they fell to mention it to me, but you already know me and Mrs. Baxter don't get along so…….. Anyway let me run this bath water for Owen babe, we got a long day ahead of us tomorrow, and I need him to help me with a few things in our yard for the competition. Oh……I disconnected the phone because someone keeps hanging up every time I answer it.

Morning came and (man-o-man) that was the longest night of my life, having to patrol the house waiting for Mr. Baxter to call or even stop by and ring the doorbell cause of my guilty conscience. He was making me feel like a scared little kid too afraid to come outside, as if a bully was out there waiting to beat me up and take my lunch money. I ran over to the window to see if the Baxter's car was in the drive way, but once again it was not there. After so long it got to the point where I start feeling like (Fuck All That)!! I'm a grown ass woman, and I made a mistake, so if I get exposed then so be it. I'm going outside to work on my garden for the big event this evening. Owen and I made our way outside, but honestly I couldn't stop looking at the Baxter's house still a little frightened. Preparing my yard for about 2-hours I couldn't take the anticipation no longer, I had to find out what was taking Mr. Baxter so long to spill the beans on me and the Box Office movie I made. I figured I'd take Owen over there with me, just in case Mr. Baxter was still mad, he would take a look at Owen and maybe spare me the embarrassment to Julius a little later during the competition. We make our way over to the house and ring the doorbell [ding dong]. Mr. Baxter answered and I said….. "Good morning". He just giggled and replied…. "No no no, that's my brother, he's at the hospital with his wife, she had surgery last night and she didn't pull through! I'm waiting on him to come home now, I talked to him earlier and I could hear in his voice that he is devastated. My brother needs me more than ever right now, but did you want to leave a message for him in case he calls back"? Oh no no…I am sorry for you guys loss, Mrs. Baxter was a good woman. I knew her for some years now, and I would never have thought this would happen to her, especially today out of all days. She looked forward to our Annual Garden Competition every year, and now she's gone I can't believe it. Me and Owen walked back home slow as a turtle, still not believing the news I just received from the twin brother. After that time just flew by, and the competition was taking place. It didn't even seem important anymore after my honorable advisory was no longer in the picture, I felt like shit……. Julius and Owen was in my corner while the judges critiqued my garden with their clipboards giving me points I didn't even earn with honor. I glanced over at the Baxter's house, and all the lights were off, and their garden was still destroyed from what my petty ass did too it a couple days ago. As the judges totaled up the points for the new winner of the Competition, to know amazement they said my name "Torri Castle" as the 1st Place Winner! I threw on the fakest smile I could conjure up, with hugs & kisses from Julius and Owen that I desperately wanted a week ago, but now is eaten me up inside. The guilt was eaten me alive, and I just couldn't take it anymore….. I stood up in front of everyone and announced; "I would like to dedicate this Award & Ribbon to Mrs. Baxter who is no longer with us due to a bad surgery last night, I know deep down if she competed today, she would have won with flying colors like she does every year. So let me place this award on her garden because this is exactly what she would have wanted"!! Everyone looked so confused….. not remembering I was the only person in the neighborhood that knew about her departure from the twin brother. I ran in the house crying my eyes out after my big speech, wishing I could have spoken to her one last time without anger in my voice, but just as a neighbor borrowing sugar, flour, or butter like normal people. Ironically, our doorbell rang about 4:00am, and I'm thinking somebody must have the wrong address because this is very disrespectful being at someone's door this late. I get out of bed headed to the front door, look through the peep hole and I see Mr. Baxter standing on the porch. Awww shit I think to myself….. it's finally time to face the music, and just my luck Julius is coming toward the front door as well. Julius answered the door…….

JULIUS:

Hey Mr. Baxter, it's kind of late but I heard about what happened to your wife and you have our condolences.

MR. BAXTER:

Well…. that's why I'm here Mr. Castle, my family and I wanted to thank your wife for the award she left on our front yard earlier this evening. We just got back from the hospital and wanted to thank you as soon as possible.

JULIUS:

I understand, and I know your wife was with us in spirit during the entire competition. Torri is still shaken up from the horrible news, and been crying all night. She's right here if you would like to speak to her, but excuse me real quick Mr. Baxter I think the doorbell must of woke up Owen, let me check on him.

TORRI:

I am so sorry for your loss Mr. Baxter, and I feel terrible about how I behaved inside home depot the other day. I pray you can forgive me.

MR. BAXTER:

I'm going to make this short & sweet while your husband is in the other room. I told my brother about your little video tape you made of him and his husband. So earlier when you spoke with him at my house, we decided to play a trick on you as well.

TORRI:

I'm confused....(as I wiped my tears from my face)

MR. BAXTER:

I could explain it to you, but I'll rather show you instead.

MRS. BAXTER:

How you doing Mrs. Castle

TORRI:

I almost passed the fuck out from shock, but instead I yelled out "ghost ghost"!!

MRS. BAXTER:

Stop all that yelling little girl, I ain't no damn ghost! I was in the hospital for surgery on my toe, but once my husband told me about your little detective blackmail scheme, we decided to teach your ass a lesson. I told my husband not to tell Julius about this because I would rather beat you at your own game.

MR. BAXTER:

Let's go honey, you need to rest your foot and get some food in your belly, I think she learned her lesson. I'm heading over to the house, so finish this up and come on sweetheart.

MRS. BAXTER:

Ok, I'm right behind you dear......Come here Torri let me whisper something to you.

TORRI:

What is it Mrs. Baxter?

MRS. BAXTER:

I didn't get a chance to compete in the Garden Competition, and still won 1st Place thanks to your guilty conscience, so how does it feel after 5-years Torri?

TORRI:

How does what feel?

MRS. BAXTER:

How does it feel to be a 2nd Place runner up to a dead woman? (Ole Sneaky Bitch)!!!

CHAPTER 5

THE SEDUCTIVE SHRINK

JULIUS:

Once a week I'm supposed to report to therapy for my job, and so far this will be my second session with Dr. Robinson. I can't even lie, she is the sexiest therapist I ever seen in my life. If she was a man I would be dreading to sit in this damn room for 1-Hour out of my busy day, but after seeing the outfit she had on last week, I can't wait to see what she'll be wearing today. Even though I'm a happily married man, I still can't deny the fact that I make sure I spray a little extra cologne on before our session, just to see if she'll notice and hopefully I'll get a compliment for my manly scent every week we meet. Coffee in hand I knock on her office door eagerly waiting for her to answer so I can see those pretty lips say "Hello Mr. Castle welcome back"! She opens the door and says exactly what I predicted, I smile and greet her back, and then we proceed to sit down to start our hourly session.

DR. ROBINSON:

So….. Mr. Castle how are you doing today? Last week we didn't cover much while you were here, so I was hoping we could discuss a little bit of why you are scheduled to see me, but before we get into all of that, how was your weekend?

JULIUS:

I smiled with a tiny smurk on my face because I remembered what took place a couple weekends ago with me, my wife, and my babysitter. I started wondering if I should tell the truth, or should I just come up with some boring shit to say so we can change the subject and get straight to business about the real reason I'm here. Before answering I asked…. "Is everything we talk about confidential in this room Dr. Robinson"? (I would hate for any incriminating information to leave this office, and get me in trouble in the future).

DR. ROBINSON:

I assure you Mr. Castle that everything you tell me is strictly between us and only us. I'm required by Law to keep all things confidential with my patients; that includes a hush hush policy with your Captain, Co-workers, and even you're Wife. Please feel free to lay on my couch, close your eyes, and treat me like a friend you been knowing for years. (Basically someone you don't mind sharing secrets with)

JULIUS:

Ok….. You asked for it! My weekend was very interesting to say the least. My Wife and I had "Date Night" like we always do every weekend, but this night was different with a little twist.

DR. ROBINSON:

A little twist? What do you mean by that Mr. Castle?

JULIUS:

By little twist I mean to say…. we had our first threesome with our babysitter the other night. Awwww Man….. I can't believe I just told you that, I promised my wife I would keep our sex life a secret, especially speaking about this threesome business.

DR. ROBINSON:

Well..... like I told you before Mr. Castle everything you tell me is confidential, so your wife will never know what we discuss anyhow. Speaking of your wife, why don't you tell me a little bit about her.

JULIUS:

Not really much too tell..... she's a great mom to our son, she takes care of all the household needs like a homemaker should, she works out at that gym by the big shopping mall even though I don't think she's been there in about a month, and we rarely have sex but don't ask me why.

DR. ROBINSON:

Oh ok, I understand if you feel uncomfortable talking about this to me, so let's just discuss why you're in therapy in the first place.

JULIUS:

Alright, about 3-months ago I shot and killed a man & child in the line of duty. I don't have much remorse about the man because he chose his fate when he pulled what seemed to be a real rifle at the time on police officers. But the little boy's death still haunts me from time to time. It probably bothers me so much because I have a little boy of my own, and I would be heart-broken if somebody shot him to death.

DR. ROBINSON:

So why don't you feel any sympathy for the man you killed? He's a human being as well right? Just out of curiosity Mr. Castle did you or the Police Department try to contact any of their relatives?..... Maybe the little boy's Mother or Father; or maybe the man's Wife or Siblings.

JULIUS:

Neither one of them had any identification on them, so it's been hard to locate any family members that they may have. We did get the blood work back, and it showed that they had the same blood type so we know that they were Father & Son. We tried to run their finger prints but everything came back negative, which is weird especially if he's a known drug dealer. I know you said this stuff is confidential, but this still is an on-going investigation, so it's kind of against the law for me to be discussing with or without your hush hush policy.

DR. ROBINSON:

I understand, and I respect your code of conduct..... Looking at my watch it seems you only have 30-minutes to go, is there anything else you would like to talk about or get off your chest before I see you next week.

JULIUS:

There is one thing I'm dying to know, but it's not about my job. It's a personal question about you.

DR. ROBINSON:

Oh really..... well this might be interesting go ahead and ask.

JULIUS:

I feel embarrassed even asking this, but you said earlier….. "Treat you like a friend I've been knowing for years" right? Ok, here it goes…. "Are you a Thong or Boy-shorts kind of woman"? (sheesh) There I said it!!

DR. ROBINSON:

Oh my….. I don't think that's actually appropriate talk for a Doctor-Patient type of relationship Mr. Castle. I'm curious of why are you even interested in my under garments? (you being a married man and all)

JULIUS:

Well, last week when we had our session I couldn't help but notice the thigh high stockings you were wearing, and the whole time I was wondering…. "What kind of panties do she have on under that business skirt"! And now today you're wearing another business skirt without the thigh high stockings, so me being a nasty man with nasty thoughts on the brain, I just have to know "Thong or Boy-shorts"?

DR. ROBINSON:

Oh I see…. well let me include you on a little secret since we're in this confidentiality room. Bring your ear a little closer so I can whisper it too you. "I didn't have on any panties last week, and I don't have on any panties now"! And you want to know something else Mr. Castle…….

JULIUS:

Oh shit….. Hell yeah Miss Robinson what else?

DR. ROBINSON:

I think your hour is up! See you next week and by the way, your cologne smells delicious!!

JULIUS:

I left out of that office with the worst case of blue balls ever, my dick was harder than a diamond caught in a ice storm. At least one thing was accomplished out of this whole teasing situation….[she noticed the extra cologne I was saturated in, and now I think I might have her hooked]. Ever since me and Torri had that threesome with Amanda, I can't stop thinking what it would be like to do the same thing again with Dr. Robinson instead. The long drive home was just what I needed, having constant thoughts of next week's therapy session, wondering what Dr. Robinson was going to be wearing, and now that I know she doesn't wear any panties, it just makes this week go by even slower with more torture to my thought process. I finally get home, and Torri's on the couch watching TV. I figured I could get my cure to my blue balls problem by making sweet love to my wife trying not to think about Dr. Robinson and her teasing, panty-less demeanor. As soon as I try to get frisky with the love of my life, first thing she noticed was my semi-new cologne smell that I been wearing all day trying to seduce my therapy crush. She compliments the scent, but quickly brings the seduction to a halt with the words…… "I really want to fuck Julius, but it's that time of the month, and these cramps are killing me! Can we just lay on the couch and watch TV while you hold me"?? I replied…. Of course my little love muffin what we watching tonight? (But on the inside I was heated like a motherfucker) I'm horny as hell, and now my blue balls done turned purple!! Anyhow…. after that nut-less night, the rest of the week dragged like a bad muffler on a broken down Chevy. Those next 7-days felt like 70-days, but before I knew it…. (Therapy Day) was finally here at last. My suit was pressed, my shoes were shined, and my infamous cologne was perfected to the "T"!! I build up the courage to knock on her office door [like I actually have a choice in the matter anyway, seeing I have to do these therapy sessions as part of my rehab for my Policemanship] And there she was, my Therapist Temptress ready to greet me with that same quote she always says coming off those pretty lips she possess….. "Hello Mr. Castle welcome back" (Ahhhhh) I think to myself (Music to my ears baby)

DR. ROBINSON:

Go ahead and take a seat sir, we'll begin in a moment.

JULIUS:

She was wearing an all white blouse, all white short pencil skirt, all white heels, and all white thigh high stockings that I could see while her legs was crossed once again. Her hair was pinned up coming off her neck with a pencil stuck in it at the back of her head I guess to keep her hair from falling. Also a pair of clear frame glasses, and every time she stopped writing on her clipboard she nibbled on her ink pen with the front of her teeth leaving red lipstick residue all over the writing utensil. Talk about the starter kit for "The Sexiest Librarian" on the fucking planet. If I ever gave her too much credit for being a goddess before today, she most definitely lived up to the godly goddess compliments while wearing all white today.

DR. ROBINSON:

Before we get started Mr. Castle I'd like to talk about the last conversation we had last week before you left my office.

JULIUS:

I already know Doc….. It was very unprofessional of us too talk in that manner, and it would be best for both parties if we just kept the sessions business orientated. I apologize for my vulgar question, and it will never happen again.

DR. ROBINSON:

Actually I was going to ask you a question this time.

JULIUS:

Oh ok, and what is that Miss Robinson?

DR. ROBINSON:

Come close so I can whisper it too you......Take a wild guess what color my Boy-shorts are today? And if you guess right, I'll go lock my office door, close the blinds, and you can do whatever it is you want to do to me for 1-Full Hour Mr. Big Daddy Castle! Oh and by the way "Your cologne smells delicious"!!

JULIUS:

Damn Dr. Robinson, your perfume smells delicious as well. So.....1-guess huh? And if I get it wrong then what happens?

DR. ROBINSON:

If you guess wrong, then you have to sit here for a whole hour like a good boy horny as fuck, and tell me how your weekend was with your boring old wife, who probably didn't give you any pussy at all poor baby! (giggle) Not to mention you're going to stare at my thigh high stockings for an entire hour, hoping that I cross my legs just one time so you can get a peek of my pretty pussy hiding behind these thin, tight, color-unnamed boy-shorts, that just so happen to be riding all in between my ass & pussy lips right now as we speak. [giggles] So are you ready to play the guessing game Mr. Castle?

JULIUS:

Alright doctor….. or Miss Robinson since your nasty [laughs] I'll play this little game with you. I assume you're an intelligent woman, so this mind game you're playing I'm sure you just already know which color I'll pick huh? You made sure you wore all white today, so the average man or should I say typical man would pick white boy-shorts thinking you would stick to the color scheme, but you told me last week that you don't wear panties at all. The one thing that you seemed to forget though is that I'm a detective Dr. Robinson, so I know exactly what color panties you're wearing.

DR. ROBINSON:

Someone seems confident huh? Ok then Mr. Castle which one is your final answer out of those two choices…. White or None?

JULIUS:

Neither! The color boy-shorts that your covering that pretty pussy behind is "RED"!!! (Final Answer)

DR. ROBINSON:

Oh My God….. There's no way you could have known that!

JULIUS:

[Smiling with confidence] Actually it's the perfect choice….. the all-white was a throw off to the average man, but your red lipstick gave you away. Your flaw is that you're a color coordinating type of woman, so you being the typical woman that has to coordinate that lipstick with something on your body….. I know you couldn't help yourself when you got dressed this morning. And your panties are the only thing that's not in plain view, so It was sort of a no brainer. [wink]

DR. ROBINSON:

Hmmmm…... Well alright Officer, a deal is a deal! How do you want to spend the rest of your session while I lock this door?

JULIUS:

As soon as she walked over to lock the door, I approached her from behind with my hands on her waist, and my lips on her ear. I slid both hands downward to the top of them sexy white thigh highs, and raised that skirt up so slow & gently until I seen the bottom of her ass cheeks hanging out those red laced boy-shorts. I immediately pulled those down to her ankles, and watched her step out of them with those white heels still on her feet. I picked them up off the floor and smelled the sweet aroma right in the crotch part. I pulled her over to her paper filled desk, and knocked every item she had on the desk onto the floor. She assumed that she was going to get bent over on the desk like you see in the movies, but I had to re-assure her that…... I'm the one that won our little bet from the guessing game, so I sat my ass on the desk, placed her in between my legs, put the palm of my hand on the top of her head, then eased her down to her knees so she could suck on this dick with those sexy lips I've grown to love these last past weeks. She grabbed my dick with those therapeutic hands, lifted it up, and start licking & sucking my ball sack while stroking my 9-inch. Her mouth was so warm, and the eye contact we made while she was down there was pure bliss. With no time to waste, she inserted the head of my penis in her mouth, using that tongue like I was an ice cream that was about to melt licking every inch of my shaft slurping spit like it was no tomorrow. In & out of her mouth back & forth picking up speed with each deep throat, I pinched her nose closed so she couldn't breathe making her breathe out of her mouth while that big dick blocked her airway. I told her that I would remove my hand from her nose to breathe only if she could make my dick touch the back of her throat like a good girl. I forced this cock all the way down her esophagus, and watched her eyes water like a cry baby that just got put in time out. Quickly I pulled my cock out of her mouth and let her take a couple breath's since she been such a good girl servicing daddy Castle's love stick. I smack it all over her face..... lips, eyes, cheeks, forehead, and nose! She looked up at me with those watery eyes, and said..... "Is daddy gone bend me over my desk, and fuck the shit out of me"? I use my hand and lift her up by her chin softly starring at those pretty tits that I mistakenly neglected this whole time. Both hands on her soft ass while she stands in front of me, I nibble, lick, and suck on her breast not missing a single piece of skin all over her chest. Her ass crack was soaking wet on my fingers, and she loved every minute of it. I then bent her over the desk kissing her arched back while my dick just sat at the top of her ass poking her spine, I then whisper in her ear during these kisses on her neck..... "You ready for Mr. Castle to fuck your little tight hole now"? She replied.... "Yes Julius Yes Julius, please stick it in me, my pussy is throbbing for that cock"!! I then start jacking off so rapidly still kissing her ear and licking her neck, then it happened (BOOM BOOM BOOM)..... I bust all over her back & ass drenching her with cum.

DR. ROBINSON:

(Breathlessly) Why did you do that Mr. Castle, I didn't even get a chance to feel you inside me?

JULIUS:

I whispered in her ear while I pulled up my pants....." I think our hour is up Doctor Robinson, see you next week, and by the way [Your Head Game was Delicious]!!!

CHAPTER 6

WORK-OUT BUDDIES

TORRI:

After all that drama I brought upon myself during the "Garden Competition", I need to relieve some stress and I'm talking Asap. My plan for today is to drop Owen off at the Daycare Center, and immediately go to the gym for a little work-out and spa-treatment to spoil myself..... (hey why not)! I would have went sooner but I been waiting on my period to end which seems to have took forever, and I'm sorry but I do not feel comfortable lifting my legs and exercising in public knowing all of that is going on down there, just feels nasty and it makes me want to stay home until mother nature runs her course. I must admit though, I had a little nasty horny moment the other day when Julius came home from his therapy session. Even though I was on my cycle, he came in the house smelling so good (I guess he bought some new cologne or whatever) I was just laying on the couch watching TV relaxing, but I had these cramps in my stomach so bad, I don't think I could have took his dick even if I wanted too that day. But my baby wasn't tripping, he let me cuddle up under him while we watched TV and we fell asleep like a beautiful couple. Welp...... "Up & Attem" like I always say, just dropped Owen off now all I need is some gas, and I'm heading downtown to the gym. I love that fitness place because it's right by the mall, so it's like a 2-in-1 type of thing. I can work-out and then go shopping right after, that is if I'm not too sore afterwards, but tell you the truth.... "I am never too tired to shop" [laugh]!! Sadly though..... this time around is going to be strictly exercising

46

no shopping, because I have to reimburse our bank account after I overly spent $350.00 dollars the other day at fucking home depot!!! Walking in the gym after a month I felt pumped, remembering some of the old faces I use to sweat with, and a few hot body employees that still work there also. I figured I'd start off slow trying not to over do things on my first day back, so I hop on the treadmill with my headphones and just jam away. About 15-minutes in my work-out I felt a (tap tap) on my shoulder from a woman that's working out just like me. "Excuse me, is your name Torri Castle"? I respond back…. "Yes I am, do I know you"? She said…. "No, I just found this credit card on the ground next to your machine, and figured it must be yours". "Why thank you, what is your name"? I would tell you mine but it's obvious you already know it [giggle].

EVA:

My name is "Eva", nice to meet you. So do you come too this gym often?

TORRI:

Well yes and no (giggles)! I used to be a regular, but I haven't been here in about a month. I'm surprised my membership still worked honestly.

EVA:

I know what you mean. This is my first time, but I used to go to another gym across town about a year ago. It's near the airport about 20-minutes away from here.

TORRI:

Oh yeah, I heard about that one. I hear it's very nice. As a matter of fact, I think that's the one my babysitter goes too.

EVA:

Oh ok, so you have kids huh?

TORRI:

Oh no…. I only have 1-kid (laughing) I have a 4-year old son his name is Owen. I been thinking about having another one cause I really want a daughter, but I don't think my husband is ready for changing diapers and making bottles again right now.

EVA:

That sounds great! Do you want to go over to the Juice Bar and grab a smoothie? It's my treat……

TORRI:

Sure why not, I only been on the treadmill for about 15-minutes and I'm kind of thirsty anyway. Let's go….. so do you have any kids?

EVA:

Naw……I wouldn't mind having one, but I have a demanding job, and not to mention I haven't found the right guy for something of that caliber just yet. So are you married, or you just got the ole baby daddy story going on? [Laugh] Oh My God….. Please forgive me, I don't mean to pry in your business like that, seeing that we just met and all.

TORRI:

(Giggles) Trust me its fine, between me and you I'm usually the one that's in other people's business. But to answer your question (Yes I'm

Married)!!! Earlier you said that your job was demanding….. What is it that you do for a living?

EVA:

I work at a hospital. And believe it or not, everybody tells me their business in that damn place [laugh] You would probably love it. Hey….. it's a shopping center next door would you like to accompany me over there? I saw a handbag in the window that's too die for!

TORRI:

I promised myself that I would do more exercising then shopping today, but what the hell I'll just do a little window shopping and watch you buy something instead.

EVA:

Cool….. let's go check out those purses & sun dresses then.

TORRI:

Wow…. this is a nice store. I didn't know they sold clothes as well, I thought they just sold purses & accessories. I wish I had some extra money on me, I think my husband would love to see me in that black lingerie outfit over there hanging up on the wall.

EVA:

Oh yes girl….. That is very sexy! I think the pink one would look better on you it matches your skin complexion better. You should go try it on in the dressing room. Let's both go, I'll try on the black one in the dressing room next door to yours.

TORRI:

Ok, what the hell….. it's not like I'm buying it anyway, so the promise I made about "No Shopping" still stands.

EVA:

Right on girl, and it don't matter anyhow, we'll just take some pictures in the outfits and if we like them, I'll just buy them for us.

TORRI:

Oh No Eva, I can't let you do that! Oh shit…. speaking of phones I left my cell in the car inside my purse. I don't like to bring my purse inside the gym, so I usually just put My I.D., credit card, and i-pod in my bra when I work-out. That's probably how I dropped my credit card earlier when you found it, these little B-cup tits I got [laugh] it probably just slid right pass my little mesquitoe bites.

EVA:

Well they look pretty plump to me, let's see how there going to look in that pink lingerie outfit. And long as your husband likes them (Fuck It)!!

TORRI:

While trying on my lingerie I could hear Eva in the stall next to me singing/humming some song that the store was playing on the intercom ceiling. The dressing room was similar to a bathroom stall with the bottom wall cut out, so I could see some of her clothes on the floor, and a glimpse of her toes as well. I loved the way the lace & silk felt on my skin as I tried on the little pink number, thinking to myself how much Julius would love to see my cute little tits and juicy ass in this pretty piece Eva picked out for me. Looking at myself in the mirror I was very pleased with the outcome, but my opinion wasn't enough. I wanted Eva to take a look and give me her honest opinion. We both walked out of the dressing rooms at the same time, and once my eyes gazed upon her I felt like the gayest person on the face of the planet. That black lingerie fitted her to perfection (Oh MY God) her breast were so pretty, and her curves from her stomach to her thighs were fucking gorgeous! We made eye contact for a brief second, and I quickly looked away hoping she didn't notice my homosexual tendencies I was thinking in my head. I told her that black is definitely her color and she definitely should buy that for any future date or lucky guy she may come in contact with later in life.

EVA:

Stop it girl…. your just saying that. Well I guess I was right though.

TORRI:

Right about what?

EVA:

Your tits do look good and plump in this pretty piece I picked out for you. I told you pink was your color, I'm buying this for you Torri!

TORRI:

No No No, I told you I can't let you do that! Let's just take some pictures like we said we we're going to do.

EVA:

I'm not buying it for you, I'm buying it for your husband. After seeing your beautiful body in this I know he'll appreciate all you do for him as a housewife. And if he doesn't appreciate it, you could always wear it for me (Hahahah) just kidding!

TORRI:

(While she playing, I really would wear it for her and Julius) But I just laughed and said… "Girl quit playing", and then hurried up and went back in the dressing room.

EVA:

A girl….. you forgot to take the picture of you wearing the outfit. Here I'm about to hand you my phone from under the stall so you can take that Sexy Selfie.

TORRI:

I was so captivated by Eva's body that I totally forgot about that damn picture. I responded….. "Oh yea I almost forgot, ok send the phone over". Her hand crept underneath the stall with the phone in her palm, and our finger tips touched gently & slowly.

EVA:

By the way Torri….. Don't scroll through my pictures, because I got a lot of naked ones in there I don't want anyone to see (Hahaha).

TORRI:

As soon as she said that, I went straight to her gallery with my gay ass. I thought that black lingerie she had on was something; (shiiiiid) her naked ass was so fucking addictive I couldn't keep my mouth closed. Then

I looked down under the stall, and there was Eva's head looking up under my stall.

EVA:

I caught you! You supposed to be taking a selfie missy, what are you looking at in my phone? Ummmmm, by the way you have a pretty pussy from down here.

TORRI:

(Stuck for words) I just start studdering...... "Oh, I'm not looking at nothing I was trying to find your camera".

EVA:

Liar Liar......(giggles) It's ok if you look at me in my birthday suit, I'm looking at you in yours right now damn near, and I'm enjoying the view from down here I must admit.

TORRI:

Oh really..... Well you better get your head from under my stall before I give you a up close & personal view right in your face.

EVA:

Don't tease me with a good time girl..... (I Dare You)!

TORRI:

You better quit playing with me Eva, I'm serious.... I'll sit on your face in this public dressing room!

EVA:

I Double Dare You!!

TORRI:

I walked over to her face while it was laying on the carpet right underneath my stall, and squatted down on her face like it was a public toilet that I didn't want to touch the seat. She stuck her tongue inside my pussy like it was a moist dick, and I rode it just the same. Up and down I bounced on her face making it hard for her to breathe as I grinded my pussy on her mouth, and my asshole on her nose. I couldn't believe what I was doing in this damn dressing room with this woman I just met at the gym, but I had a taste for cream of pussy and I'm going to make sure I get what I want. As I rose off of her face, you could see spit & slob stringing from my pussy onto her lips and it turned me on so fucking bad. I told her to move her head so I could stick my head under the stall just like she did for me. As I lay on the carpet in my dressing room, I slid my head under her stall trying my best not to mess up my hair at the same time. Once I get my head up under there, I looked up and see Eva still wearing that black lingerie that I seemed to like so much earlier. Instead of facing forward to squat on my face, she sat reverse cowgirl like she was about to get bent over by my tongue. Immediately my tongue went straight in her tight ass, and honestly this was the first time I ever ate ass before. It was so erotic, and I admit I enjoyed it a lot more then my tongue in some pussy. Forcing my tongue in a tight wet hole that suppose too be exit only made my pussy so wet, but I ignored the taboo, and stuck my finger in my own ass also. Licking ass while fingering my ass was a different experience, not to mention we're in a public place just made it more taboo. As she rocked back & forth I found myself licking ass and licking pussy all at once going from one hole to another while she moaned and grinded my face. Then…… [knock knock] somebody was at our dressing room door; (A Ladies Voice Spoke Out) "Is there someone in this stall"? Forgetting where we were being caught up in the moment, I replied….. "Yes it is, I'll be out in just a moment". (Oh My God) What if that lady would have opened up the door instead of knocking, I would have been so embarrassed. Me and

Eva quickly took off our lingerie outfits, put them back on the hanger, threw our gym clothes back on, and exited the dressing room laughing & giggling like two little school girls. We get outside the store and honestly I can't even look her in the eyes knowing all the nasty shit we just did in there.

EVA:

Hey girl.... I just want you to know that I never ever did anything like that before, and if you never want to see me again I understand. You seem uncomfortable, so from now on I'll just go to that other gym near the airport where you said your babysitter goes.

TORRI:

Naw Eva, I'm not tripping. I'm just still a little nervous from that lady knocking on our dressing room door........(OH SHIT) Babysitter!! That reminds me, I have to go and pick up my son from daycare..... what time is it, I left my phone in the car.

EVA:

Its 3:00pm, is everything going to be alright?

TORRI:

(Oh My God) I'm an hour late, I'm sorry I have to go right now!

EVA:

Ok I understand, give me your number so we can work-out again one day in the future.

TORRI:

Ok text me a little later! BYE

EVA:

Ok girly be careful.

TORRI:

As I rush and run to my car in the parking lot, I can't believe I lost track of time like that. Fucking with this bitch I just met on some homo shit, I should be ashamed of myself. Now I might have a possible Child Protective Service case on my hands cause of this encounter; man I got to stop with this sneaky shit, its leading to nothing but trouble for me and my family. As I get in the car, I rumble through my purse searching for my phone, and see I have 5-missed calls, 3 from daycare and 2 from Julius. I dialed the Daycare Office as quickly as I could, but I only got there voicemail. Then I called Julius hoping he wasn't mad at me for not answering the phone, and I know he had therapy today so……..

JULIUS:

Hello…..

TORRI:

Hey babe, I lost track of time at the gym, so I'm late picking up Owen, but I'm on my way right now to get him.

JULIUS:

It's ok…. That's why I was calling you, I picked up Owen earlier. The daycare called me after they couldn't get in touch with you, so we're at home chilling waiting on you sweetie.

TORRI:

Oh thank goodness….. I was on my way up there to the daycare right now. Well I'm on my way home right now ok. I hate that you had to leave work to pick him up Bae, and I know you had therapy today so I'm speeding through traffic as we speak.

JULIUS:

Slow down Torri and take your time. Therapy was cancelled today, so I'm actually off work right now. Stop at the store on your way home and pick up some popcorn & movie, I was thinking Me, You, and Owen could have a movie night a little later if you're not too busy.

TORRI:

Ok honey, I can do that, and I'll get some beer & wine for us just in case Owen falls asleep during the movie.

JULIUS:

Alright see you in a minute boo. Bye

TORRI:

After getting all the snacks and movie from the store, I headed straight home to the 2-men in my life. Pulling up in the driveway I noticed that I didn't get a chance to wash my face after the incident me and Eva had in the dressing room. Awwww shit....... I remembered last time at the strip club when I was in the infamous VIP Room with that Exotic Dancer, Julius smelled that pussy on my face even after I wiped it clean with a moist napkin, so how am I going to explain this on me this time? (Think Torri)..... Fuck it, I already pulled up in the driveway, so I know Julius & Owen looked out the window already and saw me, and if I stay out here too much longer my husband's gone get suspicious and bring his ass out here. (Ok ok ok) I'm going in and hopefully he just won't notice. As I walked in the door Owen jumped in my arms...... "Mommy mommy your home"!! I reply..... "Hey baby", mommy is so sorry I didn't pick you up from daycare, I was at the gym and lost track of time, but I promise that will never happen again okay"! I then speak to Julius..... "Hey babe, I'm sorry again" hoping he didn't want a kiss, but as he approached me, [like a husband should] I quickly wrap my arms around him and give him the biggest/tightest hug a wife could give her soul-mate. I whisper in his ear so seductively..... "Hmmmm I missed you so much my King (while licking his ear) to my pussy is throbbing for you so bad, that's why I rushed home"!! I'm about to go in the bathroom and wash all this sweat off of me from my work-out......while I'm in there, can you put that movie on for Owen and then meet me in our bedroom for a little one on one playtime with your naughty wife?? Before he could even answer, I un-wrapped my arms from around him, kissed him on the cheek, and hurried to the bathroom before my damn face could expose my trifling ass. Once in the bathroom I ran me some bath water and just stared at myself in the mirror in disgust. I don't know if Julius noticed the smell or not, and honestly I deserve to be exposed after my actions today at the gym. I sat in the tub and soaked my body trying to get Eva's scent off of me. I scrubbed & scrubbed my face continuously until there was nothing left. After a hour or so in the tub my entire body was wrinkled; but I still felt dirty. Alright let me get out of this bathroom and keep my promise to my hubby I was thinking, plus I still have to make dinner before it gets too late. Walking out the bathroom I notice Julius & Owen sleep on the couch with popcorn scattered everywhere, and the movie still playing. I smiled for a quick second thinking..... "Ok, I got away with this gym incident [bullet dodged]" but then I started thinking how I just missed out on Family Time with my boys cause of my sneaky ways, and I just got sad and cried. "How could I let this fetish come between me and my family"? I'm such a horrible person [crying more]!! No more….. starting today I'm done with this sneaky shit, I'm done with sleeping with women, and I'm done sticking my nose in other people's business! From now on, I'm going to be the Housewife my husband wants, and the Mother my son needs no matter what!!

CHAPTER 7

THE SPECIAL GIFT

After my reality check, and the promise I made to myself last night I ended up crying myself to sleep, and before I knew it that sun was beaming through our windows bright & early the next morning. We all feel asleep about 7:00pm yesterday, and today was just like every other morning….. cartoons, breakfast, and the smell of coffee. Julius gives me a kiss followed by Owen right after, and their off to work and school like a normal family. I figured I'd do the dishes and clean the house since everyone was gone for the day. I turn the radio on so I can get too it, blocking everything out, remembering the promise I made and said "I'm A New Woman Today"! About 2-hours into my cleaning session I see my phone flashing while sitting on the charger, thinking it's probably Julius calling to tell me how much he loves me!! But this was a number I never seen before, I answer the phone [Hello]

EVA:

Hello, can I speak to Torri

TORRI:

This is she, who is this?

EVA:

This is Eva, you rushed out of the mall so fast yesterday I was just calling to make sure you were ok.

TORRI:

[Thinking to myself]….. Just when I said I was about to change my life around, now this bitch calling me (Fuck)! I reply back…. "Oh hey girl, yea everything is fine, my husband picked up my son yesterday so I just panicked for no reason".

EVA:

Oh alright, well just to let you know I went back in that store after you left and bought both of those Lingerie Outfits we were trying on. I hope you're not mad, but I really think your hubby would like it. Just accept it as a gift, please don't tell me I wasted my money girl.

TORRI:

Awwww Eva, I told you not to buy me nothing. I feel weird accepting a gift from you seeing that we just met and all.

EVA:

I told you it wasn't a problem, so can you come and pick up this outfit before I have to mail it to you girl (Laugh)

TORRI:

[Laughing]…. You don't have to mail it girl, I'll come get it. Where do you want to meet up at?

EVA:

Well….. I'm working out of my house today on the laptop, just stop by when you get a chance, but I'm available at 2:00pm if you're not busy.

TORRI:

Ok, I'll leave out about 1:30pm. Just text me your address.

EVA:

Alright I'll be waiting

TORRI:

After I hung up the phone I was so confused. Should I just ignored her call and say fuck her and that lingerie outfit, or should I go pick it up and look at the situation a different way; On one hand you got a free $100.00 outfit for Julius, and since I already spent $350.00 at home depot, I could always make Julius believe I spent that money to make him happy instead. I mean, once I got the clothing from Eva, I could just drive off and never answer my phone again for her….. it's not like she knows where I live or anything like that so fuck it!! Okay I'm going to go get it for the sake of my marriage. 1:00pm came around and sure as shit Eva texted me the address, so I texted back "I'm on my way". I must admit though, riding through her neighborhood looking for her house, it was a very luxury neighborhood. I guess working at the hospital really pays off. I finally found the address and parked the car. As I got closer to her front door I could tell this was the right address, because I could smell her perfume on the doorstep, and it just made me reminisce about our little encounter at the mall. I had second thoughts about ringing the doorbell, because her perfume smell alone start making my kitty-kat moist, and I promised myself last night that my family was more important than any fetish I may have, and I'm not risking them anymore. So proudly I turned around to leave the porch, and then I hear the door knob turn open.

EVA:

Hey girl, did you have trouble finding the place?

TORRI:

I played it off as smooth as I could… "Oh hey girl, I thought I had the wrong house for a minute". [fake giggle]

EVA:

Nope this is it, come on in. Would you like some wine?

TORRI:

I was so nervous, I answered yes! Thinking the alcohol would probably ease my nerves, and I could be just a regular woman drinking wine with another regular woman. She gave me a glass of chardonnay and then I noticed an ashtray on the coffee table. Now that I'm a little more relaxed, I sit down on the couch and say….. "Damn Eva, I didn't know you smoked cigarettes.

EVA:

Ugh Torri I don't….. those things will kill you! But I do smoke weed from time to time, (shiiiid) after dealing with the people at my job for 12-hours, weed seems to be the only outlet. I was about to spark this joint if you want to hit it.

TORRI:

I haven't smoked that shit since high school child. I actually just came to pick up the lingerie, and then I have to pick Owen up at 3:00pm. I definitely can't do a repeat of yesterday, I almost got caught up like you wouldn't believe.

EVA:

I am so sorry about that, like I told you yesterday I never did anything like that before, and especially in a public place. Pass me that lighter next to you. Have you ever had a shotgun?

TORRI:

Oh no… I don't use guns I'm frightened of them.

EVA:

No girl [laughing]…. A shotgun from smoking! I'll inhale the smoke from the joint, and then you open your mouth while I blow it in your mouth.

TORRI:

Oh my bad [laughing]….. I feel stupid for saying that gun thing now. But to answer your question (No) I haven't.

EVA:

Open your mouth Torri…….

TORRI:

I wanted to say "No thank you" but her lips we're so fucking glossy & seductive I submitted to her without even putting up a fight.

EVA:

See that wasn't so bad, now was it?

TORRI:

After 5-10 minutes, I don't know if it was the wine or the weed, but the room started spinning and my coochie was soaking wet. All I could think about was (Damn weed make you feel like this) I would love to share this experience with Julius, but his goody too shoe detective ass would never get stoned with me. Now it started to make sense why I liked Eva so much; She was my bad girl, just like women like bad boys growing up. Before I knew it, Eva was pulling my leggings down from my waist while I laid helplessly on her comfortable couch high as hell. Honestly even if I wasn't high I think I still would have let her pull my pants down any damn way. In my head when I made that family promise last night, I actually meant "I wouldn't initiate any homosexual behavior, but if someone else initiated it, then I wouldn't be held accountable". Ok ok…. I admit it, I'm a whore and proud of it!! I lifted my ass up a little off the couch and let her peel my leggings all the way off like a banana, and right after that she started kissing & licking my pussy right through my panties. That teasing tongue of hers had me so ready, but she wouldn't take off my panties.

EVA:

Don't you move Mrs. Torri, I'll be right back, I have a surprise for you.

TORRI:

I thought she was going to get the lingerie she promised me, but when she came back out it was something else in her hand instead. What is that you got Eva?

EVA:

It's called a "Strap-on"! How big is your husband's dick Torri?

TORRI:

He's about 9-inches give or take, but that's huge what size is that thing?

EVA:

This is 11-inches would you like to try something Bigger & Better?

TORRI:

I wanted to say no, but seeing that big dick strapped around her waist, knowing that wet cunt was underneath, and them big tits all on the same woman, I couldn't even speak. I let her stick that fake cock in me, and all I could do was scream as it entered my purring kitty. She shoved it in there back & forth so roughly I felt like I was being raped, and now once again I found a New Fetish I was into and didn't have the slightest idea I was interested in. Her hands went around my throat as she fucked me, and the thought of being taken advantage of on some rape shit had me creaming all over that dildo. I moaned and moaned but that just made Eva go deeper & harder. I guess she was getting pleasure from using that toy on me, because soon as I yelled out "Oh Shit Oh Shit I'm about to cum"! She yelled out the same thing, and we both climaxed at the same time. I was exhausted after that sexual beating so I closed my eyes, and ended up falling asleep right there on the couch. I don't remember how long I was sleep, but I was awoken by a man standing over me in a suit and tie. He tapped me as I woke up and said.... "Excuse me Miss, what are you doing here"? In shock I tried to cover up my naked body saying.... "Oh my god, who are you and where is Eva"? He looked confuse as he replied.... "Who is Eva? My name is Anthony Logan, and I'm a Real Estate agent showing this house at 5:00pm today. Are you here for the Open House"? Now I'm really confused...... (Open House)?? Awwww shit did you say it was 5:00pm? I hurried up and found my clothes laying there on the floor and quickly got dressed. As I looked at my phone it was 4:30pm, and once again I was late picking up Owen at daycare. I ran out of the house as fast as lightening, jumping in my car assuming Julius picked up Owen, and once again I looked like a horrible neglecting parent. I called Julius already with an apologetic tone in my voice, and he answered....

JULIUS:

Hey baby, what's up?

TORRI:

Hey honey, I'm sorry you had to pick up Owen again, I got stuck in traffic down here by the airport at this new Fitness Club.

JULIUS:

What are you talking about Torri? I didn't pick up Owen today, I'm still at work.

TORRI:

What? Oh ok, well he must still be there waiting on me. I'll call you back.

JULIUS:

Ok, call me back.

TORRI:

Ok bye….. I called the daycare as soon as I hung up with Julius. [Ring ring] They answered: "Hello"….. Hello this is Torri Castle Owen's mom, I'm running late but I'm on my way right now!! [they spoke back]….. "Oh hello Mrs. Castle, Owen has already been picked up, A lady name Amanda said she was his babysitter, so we let him leave with her. She was listed on your emergency contacts so……… We tried to call you and your husband, but all we got was the voicemails. Hello hello Mrs. Castle are you there"???

TORRI:

I hung up and called Amanda immediately, but her phone was disconnected. No voicemail or dial tone. Now my heart was beating faster than it supposed to, and my hands wouldn't stop shaking at the steering wheel. (What the fuck is going on)!!! Ok calm down Torri, maybe there at the house waiting on me to get there, and I'm just being paranoid as usual. I get home after about 15-minutes speeding through traffic like a bat out of hell, run inside the house like a crazy woman looking for Owen & Amanda. After checking every room in the house I just walk on the front porch, fall to my knees and scream while crying….. (God what have I done, what have I done)!! I look up and see Mrs. Baxter waving from her porch trying to get my attention…..

MRS. BAXTER:

Torri Torri……I have a package over here with you guys name on it, I guess our mail got mixed up again. Sorry I can't personally drop it off to your doorstep like you did ours that one day. [giggles]

TORRI:

Yeah yeah whatever Mrs. Baxter, I'm not in the mood for sarcasm today bitch, I'm looking for my son!!

MRS. BAXTER:

Bitch……. once my toe heals I'll show you a real bitch!!

TORRI:

Then Amanda's car pulled up in the driveway and I can see Owen playing in the backseat with one of his toys just as innocent as can be. They both get out the car and walk on the porch like nothing even happened.

AMANDA:

Mrs. Castle are you alright, looks like you've been crying? The daycare contacted me after you and Julius didn't answer. We went to that gym near the airport hoping to surprise you, because that's where Owen said you were last time you didn't pick him up. I guess you were at the gym next to the big shopping center instead.

TORRI:

Right right, of course…… I was at the gym losing track of time just like yesterday. I need to start bringing my phone inside from now on, because anything can happen while I'm in there. Why is your phone disconnected? I tried calling you earlier to thank you for picking up Owen.

AMANDA:

My phone isn't disconnected, I have a new number but I don't think I gave it to you (sorry)

OWEN:

Hey mommy…. I thought you said you wouldn't forget about me again?

AMANDA:

She didn't forget about you, she sent me to pick you up instead so she could stay at the gym longer [winking at Torri] You don't want your mom to be a Fat Old Woman like Mrs. Baxter across the street now do you? [Laugh] Go put your book bag in the house so me and your mommy can finish talking.

OWEN:

Ok, see you later Amanda! Love you mommy.

TORRI:

Thank you so much for that, I really didn't mean to be late picking him up. Well I know you have things to do so, let me give you some gas money and let you go about your day.

AMANDA:

No money needed Mrs. Castle, but I been thinking a lot about that Threesome we had and I really would like for me & you to have our own private session without your husband being involved.

TORRI:

I'm very flattered, but I only do things like that with my husband. I honestly thought you were interested in him not me.

AMANDA:

[Giggling] Oh really….. your husband is very attractive, but I got a thing for pussy, and looking in your eyes that night it seemed like you do too! How about I give you my new number, and you call me when you get a chance.

TORRI:

Alright Amanda I'll do that. Now let me get in this house and help Owen get situated. I watched Amanda pull off and start thinking…… (Damn, am I in the gay world and don't even realize it? I'm already having a secret affair with this Eva woman that Julius knows nothing about, and now Amanda wants to fuck me on the low-low as well. What the hell I'm I doing with my life, this bitch Eva had me in a strange house that wasn't even hers, I still didn't get the Lingerie Outfit, and this is the 2nd time I was late picking up Owen) I need to get in the tub and think about my next move.

CHAPTER 8

THE BLACKMAIL

JULIUS:

Saturday morning at the precinct and all I see is Paperwork Paper work! That's all I seem to do at work these days. I can't wait until I'm done with these Therapy Sessions so I can get back on the streets, and stop driving this stationary desk. I'm still kind of curious why Dr. Robinson cancelled our session the other day, it's not like her to miss out on a scheduled appointment. I'm guessing she's mad about our intense meeting we had last week, and now she probably doesn't even want to help me anymore. While daydreaming about that Therapeutical Blowjob I get a phone call at my desk [ring ring] "Police Department Detective Castle speaking"

MRS. BAXTER:

How you doing Julius, this is Mrs. Baxter your neighbor.

JULIUS:

Hey Mrs. Baxter how are you. I haven't spoken to you since you had surgery and Torri thought you died in the hospital. [Laugh]

MRS. BAXTER:

[Giggles] I know! Your wife definitely has a vivid imagination. Anyway I have some mail over here at my house with your name written all over it. I would have dropped it off in your mailbox, but my toe is still a little swollen and I can't walk too far. I tried to give it to your wife the other day, but she cussed me out and went in the house.

JULIUS:

Well ok, I can pick it up once I get home if you're still going to be awake.

MRS. BAXTER:

I think you really should come right now, there's something you really need to see.

JULIUS:

Alright! [Confused] I'll be there in the next hour.

MRS. BAXTER

Please hurry, it's very important!

JULIUS:

Once I hang up I'm thinking......(what mail could be so important that I have to leave my job for, but then again it is Saturday so maybe I'll enjoy the evening weather, take a hour lunch break real quick and see what Mrs. Baxter crazy ass wants) Then unexpectedly my Captain stops at my desk with good news….. "Hey Castle, we finally got an I.D. on that little boy and old man you killed. Their names were (Jonathan & Corey Roberts), we're running their names through the database right now for any next of kin's. It might take an hour or so, just be patient and I'll keep you in the loop". Oh man Captain that's great! Now I can get some closure to all this madness & regret I've been carrying around. I need to run home real quick and check on the house, my wife & son are out and about on this beautiful weekend, so I'm not sure if all the doors are locked up. It should only take me about an hour, and then when I get back those names should be available so we can close this case. I run to the parking lot to hop in my car happy as ever, now all I have to do is see what Mrs. Baxter is ranting & raving about, and then back to the precinct. It took me about 20-minutes to get home (or should I say to Mrs. Baxter's) I ring the doorbell but the door was already cracked open. I push it open a little more and yell….. "Mrs. Baxter it's me Julius, I'm here to pick up the mail you mentioned on the phone"

MRS. BAXTER:

I'm here in the living room, lock the door and come on in.

JULIUS:

I crept in and see Mrs. Baxter sitting on the couch in a silky gown looking very provocative, she honestly puts me in the mind of "Blanche from that old sitcom Golden Girls, but a little chubbier". I then speak….." How are you doing, I'm here to pick up the mail".

MRS. BAXTER:

Nice to see you Julius, I called you over here in such a hurry because I committed a Federal Offense! I opened up someone else's mail, and for your sake you should be glad I did.

JULIUS:

What are you talking about Mrs. Baxter? I'm on the verge of cracking a case that took me 3-months to put together. I really don't have time for games right now.

MRS. BAXTER:

Oh this is no game I assure you Mr. Castle, you might want to take a seat while I push play on this DVD Player.

JULIUS:

DVD......what are you talking about?

MRS. BAXTER:

I'm talking about this DVD that was sent to your house from a Dr. Robinson. Just your luck it got sent to my address by mistake [winks] I don't know who she is, but I'm sure your wife would love to know who she is after she sees this DVD, and you should get an award as well for your passionate role in this movie.

JULIUS:

[I'm sweating bullets now] Show me the DVD because I have no idea what you're talking about.

MRS. BAXTER:

I thought you would never ask......[Remote Clicks] Now Seeing that therapist on her knees sucking your cock on this part is just what your marriage needs Mr. Castle [laughing].......[Fast Forward] Oh and I love this part right here at the end, how you jack-off on her back and cum on her spine......I will give you credit though, because looking at that woman's beauty and for you not too have had sexual intercourse with her was very honorable; That's the real reason I didn't expose this, I respect that you only stick your dick in your wife's pussy, and not any random woman.

JULIUS:

Oh my god what the fuck!! Give me that brown package, you said Dr. Robinson sent this to me! That crazy psycho bitch!!

MRS. BAXTER:

No Mr. Castle! She sent it to TORRI CASTLE. It's funny how things happened Julius…. I actually tried to give Torri this package the other day not even knowing what was inside, but we ended up cussing each other out and she never came and got it. I dropped your package by mistake and I heard a crack noise inside, so I opened it a little bit and noticed that it was a DVD. I honestly thought it was a DVD about gardening with special tips that she might have gotten online, so I figured I would watch it and be 2-steps ahead of her for the Garden Competition next year. But once I push play all I saw was YOU & the Doctor!!!

JULIUS:

Ok Mrs. Baxter I appreciate you for recovering this for me, and we definitely can't tell anybody about this, but I need that DVD right now. I have to destroy it before anyone else sees it, especially Mr. Baxter...... awww shit did he see it?

MRS. BAXTER:

Calm down Julius, no one seen this DVD but me. My husband is at his Bowling Tournament with his brother so he won't be back until later tonight. I can't lie Mr. Castle, watching you in that recording turned me on very much. I would love to see that big dick in person!

JULIUS:

Sorry Mrs. Baxter...... like you said earlier, I only stick my dick in my wife's pussy! Remember! Anyway [snatches Dvd out] I'll be taking this DVD thank you, and no need to get up I can find my way out the door [Goodnight]!!

MRS. BAXTER:

I guess I'll just have to masturbate to the copy I made to my cellphone instead [sighs]

JULIUS:

What copy???

MRS. BAXTER:

Oh did I say that out loud [giggles]? Of course I made a duplicate Mr. Detective I need some kind of insurance to get what I want.

JULIUS:

And what is it that you want Mrs. Baxter?

MRS. BAXTER:

I want to do exactly what you and that doctor did in the DVD, except I want to play YOU and you play the doctor! See..... Mr. Baxter doesn't get hard anymore, and he refuses to get checked up at the hospital, I think he's just too proud to admit he has a problem. But in the meantime I'm the one that suffers sexually, so he can keep his pride. It's just not fair [crying] I'm supposed to stay loyal & committed as the good ole wife, but I'm burning up inside with desire, and can't do anything about it. People think 60-year old people shouldn't have sex because were old, but we feel and need passion just like the next human being. I know I'm considered a BBW and a lot of men don't like that, but I got some good pussy between these thighs I tell you that Julius!

JULIUS:

Don't cry Mrs. Baxter come here and give me a hug. I put the DVD down next to a pile of other DVD's she had laying around so I could console her. You're absolutely right, it isn't fair that you're denied love, and who doesn't like a BBW? I myself love a chunky woman with some meat on her bones, I sometimes wish Torri was a little thicker but I would never tell her that. [Laughs] Now stop all that crying on my shoulder and wipe those tears. As Mrs. Baxter wiped her tears on my shirt, she kept running her lips by my neck each time, and for a minute my dick started getting hard. She was wearing this silk turquoise gown that stopped at the waist, this sweet smelling perfume, and when I looked over her shoulder while she was on my shoulder, I could these huge ass cheeks with no panties covering them. I couldn't resist, I had to grab one of those ass cheeks, not to mention this is the only way I'm going to get the copy out of her phone, so I have to perform like a Oscar Winner tonight; just to save my marriage!

MRS. BAXTER:

Is it that ass soft Mr. Castle? It looks like your dick is about to burst through your pants, let me pull that monster out and taste it a little bit.

JULIUS:

I can't even deny it, that big soft ass booty had my dick at attention like it was in the military. She wasn't your average 60-year old lady though, she may plant flowers and bake in the kitchen, but her body was seducing me like a younger woman. Her ass looked like 2-honey baked hams, thighs thick as fuck, some Double D tits, and some full lips that would bring a dead man back to life from CPR. Funny thing is......I don't even like fat girls, but Mrs. Baxter got me horny for some BBW loving and I need that other copy as well. Fuck it..... go head and pull that monster out baby, show me how much passion you been denied! She pulled down my zipper, and stroked it slow and smooth, took her time with it just like an older woman with patience would do.

MRS. BAXTER:

Ooooooh Mr. Castle! Is all this for me baby, I hope I can fit all of it in my mouth. [Slurp slurp]

JULIUS:

My head just fell back on the couch while she sucked my cock on her and Mr. Baxter's couch. I didn't even get my pants off, she left them on my ankles and just sucked away while I laid there half naked.

MRS. BAXTER:

I hope you enjoyed that little sample Julius, but like I said earlier..... I want to play your role, and you play the doctor. You made her suck your dick in that office on the desk, you were choking her with your cock and everything, and then once you were done using her, you came on here back and then left! I want to know how that feels..... to be DOMINATE!!!

JULIUS:

[Remember Oscar winner] Oh yeah…. no problem Mrs. Baxter, lay back and let me give you a sample. I get on top of her kissing her neck and biting her ear, kissing those full lips that just came off of my penis still glossy from spit, those nipples big as cherries and her breast the size of watermelons. I licked everything that's jiggling on this woman. Then…. I creep my chin past her belly button giving it a little kiss on my way down, using my strong hands pushing her legs back from behind her knees, looks like her tits and thighs are at her neck by the way I got her thick ass wrapped up from my point of view. Only thing in my face at this point is an shaved Bath & Body Works smelling pussy, a clit the size of a Peanut M&M, and a tight booty-hole surrounded by two enormous booty cheeks. I slowly kiss her inner thighs one by one, nibbling and licking at the same time.

MRS. BAXTER:

Oh yes Julius….. lick those thick thighs, and I can feel your beard tickling my clit every time you move your head. This feels so good to be dominate, can I please have more?

JULIUS:

Only under one condition Mrs. Baxter.

MRS. BAXTER:

Yes yes I already know, I'll give you the other copy….. just please don't stop!

JULIUS:

I wasn't talking about that, but thank you anyway. The condition is…. Only if you promise to hold my head down in that pussy until you cum! I wasn't interested at first, but this blackmail thing is turning me on, not to mention I'm not use to fucking with a plus size woman, you see how small Torri is……I think you found a fetish in me that I never knew was there.

MRS. BAXTER:

So your telling me, you'll still do this even though I said I would give you the copy?

JULIUS:

[Between her legs] Lick lick….. what do you think?

MRS. BAXTER:

Oh my god…. your beard just went across my clit again! Why don't you have a closer look! [she holds her hand on his head]

JULIUS:

Ummmmm there you go Mrs. Baxter, make me eat that pussy! I push those legs back as far as her thick thighs would allow! I start off by just kissing the clit a peck at a time, then I slide my tongue across it a couple of times just to see it pulsate. I look up and see Mrs. Baxter sucking on her own nipples while I tease that pussy. I decided to put the whole clit in my mouth and just suck on it, and slob on it like it was no tomorrow!! Mrs. Baxter was going nuts twirling my head around trying her best not to break a nail, moaning like crazy, and my dick was hard and ready for some pussy.

MRS. BAXTER:

Eat that pussy Mr. Detective! This pussy haven't been slobbed down in about 10-years, take me to ecstasy Mr. Castle, be my little pussy eater while my husband is away (Yes Yes)!!

JULIUS:

She was saying all the nasty shit I wanted to hear….. I slid one of my fingers up her wet asshole while still eating that pussy, and it swallowed my finger right up in there.

MRS. BAXTER:

OH MY GOD, OH MY GOD, you found my spot Julius…. You about to make me CUM on your face……Oh Oh Oh I'm Cumming, I'm Cumming!!

JULIUS:

Her thighs trembled and shook like her whole body was in an earthquake in California. I didn't stop either…… I kept fingering that ass and eating that fat cunt until she stop shaking. After she was finish with her seizure I rose up, wipe my face with my hand, use that spit as lubrication for my dick, and then stuck my 9-inch right inside that 60-year old vagina that been denied all these years.

MRS. BAXTER:

Oh my goodness, you feel so big inside of me baby. I definitely didn't think I was going to get fucked today, ooooooh daddy keep ramming me!

JULIUS:

I sucked those tits while I fucked the shit out of her, and all I could feel was her hands & nails on my waist pulling me in her pussy with each thrust I made. My balls were smacking her asshole, and her booty cheeks was like a suction every time I pumped inside. I wanted to go longer, but something about her thickness was making me reach my peak prematurely, and I could tell it was going to be a phat nut. Oh Shit Mrs. Baxter...... Oh Shit, Oh Shit..... I pulled my dick out that slippery pussy while I was cumming at the same time!!

MRS. BAXTER:

Yes Yes.... bust that load all over me baby, drench me with that cum!

JULIUS:

Awwwww Man! That felt amazing Mrs. Baxter I know we're neighbors and all but...... [Ring ring] Goes their house phone interrupting our little Porno.

MRS. BAXTER:

Hello Hello...... Oh hey honey.... Ok..... No problem I'll see you soon.

JULIUS:

Who was that? [Jealousy voice]

MRS. BAXTER:

That was my husband duh [giggles] he's on his way home for a break while they wait on their turn to bowl. I made him some food earlier, so he wants it warmed up once he gets here. I really hate to kick you out after all of this, but I love my husband Julius, and he can't see you here. And don't worry your secret is safe with me even though I really don't like your wife. I'll delete your video in my phone, and you can take the DVD with you.

JULIUS:

Thank you Mrs. Baxter, you really are a real nice lady with some bomb ass pussy [laughs] Let me get out of here before your husband gets home. I put my clothes on quicker than a kid late for school that's about to miss the bus. Out of the Baxter's house, and into my car like a thief in the night. Once I get comfortable in the car, I throw the DVD in the passenger seat, and then I check my phone. 2-voicemails and 3-missed calls….. The Captain called twice and I see Torri called once. I check the first voicemail…..

VOICEMAIL:

[Beep] 1st New Message: Hey babe…. Me, Owen, and Amanda are at the arcade that we always take Owen too, if you get a chance to go on break come up here and check on us. [Whispers] Me and Amanda been drinking a lot of wine, so you might get lucky and get another threesome Mr. [giggle] (Love You) call me back.

VOICEMAIL:

[Beep] 2nd New Message: Castle…. this is your Captain, where are you? You said you would be only gone for an hour! Anyway the next of kin information just came through the database. Come to find out the "Old Man" you killed Jonathan Roberts was a father of 3-children and married to a Marie Roberts. Marie was killed about 6-months ago from being poisoned to death with some kind of drug only used in hospitals. Jonathan had 2-girls & 1-boy, but not anymore cause you seemed to have killed his only son. His 2-daughters are named Eva & Amanda Roberts. Call me back Asap there's more.

JULIUS:

[Dialing The Captain] Come on pick up, I knew I shouldn't have been in there fucking with Mrs. Baxter all that damn time.

CAPTAIN:

Hello….. Police Department this is the captain speaking how may I assist you.

JULIUS:

Cap…. it's me Julius. I just got your voicemail about Jonathan & Corey Roberts, we finally got a good lead on the case, I'm on my way to the precinct now.

CAPTAIN:

There's more Julius……that one name doesn't sound familiar too you?

JULIUS:

Well….. my babysitter name is Amanda, but come on now, how many Amanda's are there in this city? [Giggle]

CAPTAIN:

Holy Shit….. your babysitter name is Amanda?

JULIUS:

Yeah.... so what's the big deal?

CAPTAIN:

I wasn't talking about the Amanda name I was talking about the "Eva" name.

JULIUS:

Well I don't know any Eva's captain, your confusing me now, tell me what's going on?

CAPTAIN:

Your Therapist Dr. Robinson real name is" Eva Robinson"!!

JULIUS:

Holy Shit..... my therapist name is Eva and my babysitter name is Amanda, I'm hoping this is a huge crazy coincidence!

CAPTAIN:

Here's the kicker Castle......Their mother Marie Roberts......maiden name was (MARIE ROBINSON)!! So basically you killed Eva & Amanda's Father and Little Brother 3-months ago, and they've been plotting against you all this time I would assume. Bad part is, they haven't broken any laws or made any threats toward you or your family so there's nothing we can really do. You're the Detective Castle, time for you to finally earn your pay. I'll be on stand-by if you need me. (Good luck Officer)

JULIUS:

The phone instantly fell from my ear, how could I be so blinded. All this time these women positioned themselves in my life and my family life for the sake of revenge and I had no clue. Then I remembered that 1st voicemail..... Oh Shit, Torri's at the arcade with Amanda & Owen right now [panicking] I have to get there as soon as possible before it's too late!!

CHAPTER 9

THE CONCLUSION

TORRI:

After soaking in a hot bath the other day, I got a chance to really think my situation through. I'm going to use this Saturday to my advantage with a perfect plan I brewed up while sitting in that boiling water of a tub. This Eva chick is a dirty little bitch, and after she left me in that house the other day naked, I owe her some motherfucking payback. Owen doesn't have any daycare today, so I think I'll take him to the Big Arcade he loves to go to. It's a very nice setup, they have games, go-kart racing, skating, bowling, etc..... everything I need to keep him busy as I unfold my plan. I'm going to invite Amanda to join us, and hopefully I can get Eva there as well. I figure I can introduce them to each other, and by the way their sex drives are, they should like each other as soon as they meet. The way I see it, I can get rid of both of them [like killing 2-birds with 1-stone], and if I'm ever feeling freaky, we all can hook up on some threesome shit once every blue moon. Sooner or later they'll get tired of my motherly married ass, and eventually kick me out their little gay group and it will just be me and Julius back to normal. Owen and I get dressed about 4:00pm, and then I start calling Amanda [ring]

AMANDA:

Hello......

TORRI:

Hey Amanda, this is Torri. Me and Owen are going to the Big Arcade, I was wondering if you wanted to join us?

AMANDA:

Oh hey Torri, I don't have any classes today, so yeah I can meet you guys up there in like 30-minutes. I'm about to get out the tub, and get dressed. By the way.... did you think about what I said to you on the porch the other day?

TORRI:

As a matter of fact I did, and I really would like to hook up with you again without Julius being involved. How would you feel if I brought another beautiful woman in our circle to play with?

AMANDA:

As long as she's pretty like you, I definitely wouldn't mind having 2-pussys to play with at the same time.

TORRI:

Sounds great, I'll invite her up to the arcade as well so we all can get acquainted this evening. By the way......is that pussy wet while you're in the tub right now? [I'm so fucking gay]

AMANDA:

Actually I'm out of the tub right now, I'm sitting on my bed naked putting lotion on my body. I could stick my finger in there real quick and check for you.

TORRI:

Ooooooh yes! Check for Big Mama real quick, and put the phone down there so I can hear if it's creamy & sticky!

AMANDA:

[Fingering herself] Oh yeah big mama, it's very creamy down there, can you hear how much she missed you.

TORRI:

[Fuck!] Her pussy sounded like somebody was over there stirring up some thick ass macaroni & cheese, and they were about to put it in a pan to be baked for Thanksgiving. It sounds very delicious Amanda, I bet that bathed pussy taste so good right now!

AMANDA:

[Laugh] I just tasted it Mrs. Castle, and since I been eating pineapples & grapes all morning it has a fruity taste to it.

TORRI:

Oh my god….. let me hang up this phone before I have to fuck around and change my panties, I'll see you later at the arcade ok beautiful.

AMANDA:

Ok gorgeous, I'll see you soon. And I'll make sure I wear a skirt with no panties just in case we can get away from the public while were out. [Hangs phone up]

TORRI:

All I could do is bite my bottom lip when she said that, and the funny part is, I was already wearing a skirt as well. I'm not gone lie though, I hurried to the bathroom and pulled my panties right off after she told me she was going panty-less.

OWEN:

Come on mommy, were going to be late for the games [sighs] How long are you going to be in the bathroom?

TORRI:

I'm coming pooh, I just had to fix my make-up & hair, but I'm ready now. Come on let's go. We get in the car on this beautiful day, I roll down all the windows so we can enjoy the breeze while we cruise through the streets. Now Owen, make sure you put on your seatbelt before we pull off, you know how important that is.

OWEN:

I remember mommy, look at me I did it all by myself this time.

TORRI:

Yes you did boo, I'm so proud of you! Good job. We pull out the driveway, and once were on the road I immediately called Eva's phone [ring ring]

EVA:

Hello…. Hey girl I been waiting on your call. I am so sorry I left you the other day at my house, I had an emergency down at the hospital, and I couldn't wake you up. I probably shouldn't have given you that weed shotgun [giggle]! (Thinking to myself) [I know she must have received that Video by now of Me and Julius in my Office; Either this is a set-up, or she didn't get it in the mail yet.

TORRI:

Are you sure that was your house? I was awoken by a Real Estate agent, who said he was having an Open House at that address the same day we were there. I asked him where you were, and he looked at me confused like he didn't even know who you were.

EVA:

You must be talking about Anthony Logan, well he likes to play a lot of games so he probably tried to trick you that's all.

TORRI:

Hmmmmm……Yea maybe your right, but you still could have called me later and explained why you left me there. I'm still mad at you about that!

EVA:

Awwww poor baby, Mama can make it up to you if you like.......

TORRI:

Oh really? How about you meet me at the Big Arcade Place near the airport in an hour. I'm taking my Son up there to play, and I got someone I want you to meet.

EVA:

I'm really not interested in meeting your husband Torri, this sounds like a family type thing and I would hate to be involved in any drama.

TORRI:

[Laugh] You really think I want you to meet my husband after all the shit we've done. I think our eyes & faces would give us away in an instant! It's a friend of mine, She's a woman.

EVA:

Oh alright, I wouldn't mind meeting another woman, especially if she's a friend of yours Sexy!

TORRI:

I was hoping you would say that baby, and by the way; what are you wearing right now?

EVA:

I'm wearing a Red Dress, with some Red Heels! Why? You want to stick your face up under there and pull my panties down with your teeth?

TORRI:

I guess you'll just have to see now won't you…. And one more thing, keep all that sexy red shit on, but lose the panties boo!! (Bye) [phone hangs up] After I hung up on Eva, I start feeling more in charge of my life again. I'm not gone let these bitches run me around no more, my plan is in effect and so far working like a charm.

EVA:

No this bitch didn't just hang up on me! I hate to admit it, but I kind of liked that a little bit. Let me take these panties off just in case this isn't a set-up.

TORRI:

We finally pull up at the Big Arcade Place and Owen is so excited. As we walk inside the building, there's a huge crowd at the Bowling Alley area, I guess there's some sort of Tournament taking place today. I glance through the crowd and see Mr. Baxter ugly ass holding a bowling ball taking pictures with a team dressed in blue & red. I assume him and his gay ass brother are on a team, because there both dressed alike looking like some dip-shits [laughing]. I quickly get Owen on his favorite Car Game, and then I go order me and Amanda a glass of wine at the bar. Sitting there for about 10-minutes I see Amanda walk through the door with a little tank top that's showing off her big ass tits, and a blue jean skirt that was short as fuck. She makes eye contact with me, and strolls over toward my table where I'm sitting.

AMANDA:

Hey Torri, I was hoping you guys were already here. I didn't want to be early looking stupid waiting here with this short ass skirt on. Don't just sit there, stand up and give me a hug, let me see that skirt your wearing Miss Lady. Oh yea….. your booty looks good in this skirt Torri.

TORRI:

I was going to say the same thing about you Sexy! I'm assuming you're not wearing any panties under there, am I right?

AMANDA:

I guess you'll have to find out if you really want to know. Damn…. I almost forgot, where is Owen?

TORRI:

He's over there on that Car Game, and after that he'll jump on the Motorcycle Game [giggle] The only time he'll come over here is when he gets thirsty or hungry.

AMANDA:

Oh ok, well I see you already ordered me a glass of wine, very courteous of you Mrs. Castle [smiling] I don't know about you, but after a couple more glasses of these, my pussy is going to start dripping on my shoes, because I don't have on any panties to catch my juices.

TORRI:

Then maybe I'll have to take you in the little girl's room, bend down on my knees and help you wipe off those shoes with my tongue. I love the taste of pineapples & grapes.

AMANDA:

Oh…. so you remembered what my breakfast consisted of huh? Too bad, you're wearing panties though, I would have loved to slide this shoe off under the table, and stick my toes in between your legs and feel that moist vagina.

TORRI:

Well I guess it's your lucky day, because I'm not wearing any panties either [winks eye]! While our table was getting hot and intense from our sexual teasing, I look over toward the door and see Eva walk in…….. She was wearing a Red Business skirt, Red Heels, and some Red Lipstick, every man in the building stopped what they were doing to have a look at this bitch. She saw me and Amanda sitting at the table, and she walked right over to us.

EVA:

What's up Torri

TORRI:

Hey you Miss Show-stopper! [Laughing] I think every man in here just drooled their self when you walked in. I would like you to meet my friend Amanda, and vice versa, Amanda I would like you to meet Eva.

EVA:

Nice to meet you Amanda, I'm loving that jean skirt girl.

AMANDA:

Nice to meet you as well…. your definitely killing it with that Red Miss Thang.

OWEN:

Mommy mommy, I need to go to the bathroom! Hurry hurry, I don't want to have an accident.

TORRI:

Excuse me ladies, I'll be right back. Come on Owen let's hurry up.

EVA:

Amanda what the fuck are you doing here Little Sister? You're supposed to babysit at their house only, and give me any personal information I may need.

AMANDA:

I know, but I didn't think I would actually end up fucking Mrs. Castle [confused] I understand that you taught me everything I know sexually Big Sister, but I'm starting to get tired of this incest thing we got going on, and now I want my own girlfriend.

EVA:

Listen Little Sister….. your job was to fuck Julius, make him and Torri break-up, and then console him by making him fall in love with you. I was the back-up plan just in case he wasn't attracted to you, I could get him to fall for me instead. Do you know how hard it was for me to get assigned to his Therapy Case? And as far as the incest part go….. Me and You agreed that we would please each other sexually for the rest of our lives because there's to many diseases out here to contract, and we're the only 2-people we can trust in this world since Mom, Dad, and Corey is dead (what the fuck)!!!

AMANDA:

I'm sorry Eva, I hope I didn't mess anything up. The little boy Owen is really what distracted me. He reminds me so much of Corey, and being with their family makes me miss our family [sighs]

EVA:

Oh brother….. so now you've built a connection with them huh? So let me guess you're ready to back out of the plan that took us 4-months to prepare. Well, just to inform you…. I already sent Torri a DVD Package in the mail of Me and Julius in my office having a very good Oral Session the other day [laughing] Now that were all here, I have to push up the time table of destroying their perfect little family starting as soon as she comes out of the bathroom. I can't allow her to go home Amanda. Once she realizes that I fucked with Julius, she won't ever let me get this close again, and once Julius figures out that Me & You are the daughters of Jonathan & Marie, he'll move them away and we'll never find them again.

AMANDA:

So what is your plan Sister?

EVA:

We're going to put something in her wine, and a little something in her Son's soda that I got from the hospital. It's going to make her fall asleep for a while and then we'll see from there. We can take them to the Airport Parking Structure, and start making our demands from there.

AMANDA:

Ok Eva, just promise me that you won't hurt Owen. He's only 4-years old and never did anything to hurt anybody.

EVA:

You're so pathetic Mandy..... This Julius fucker killed our Little Brother & Father, and you still want to spare his Son after he murdered our family! I wish Mom was still alive, cause I definitely could count on her to help me destroy them after what they done to us. I can still remember me and her sitting down at the kitchen table earlier that day before she died. She loved having Tea Time with me, and I still remember how jealous you used to get every time Me and Her spent that time together. Mom almost burned her tongue off [giggles] from the Tea being so hot last time we we're together, I had to switch cups with her cause mine was semi-cooler (Man those were the days)!!

AMANDA:

I was never jealous of you and Mom, I always loved both of you, but I'm with you Big Sister through thick & thin. Whatever you want to do I know Mom's looking down on us and she would always say "Blood is Thicker than Water"!!

EVA:

Alright Little Sister, just follow my lead when she comes back and I'll take care of the rest.

TORRI:

Hurry up Owen….. we been in this bathroom for 10-minutes already I thought you said you only had to pee-pee?

OWEN:

I thought I did mommy, but I guess I had to boo-boo too!

TORRI:

Let me call your daddy, and see if he wants to stop by and join you on the Motorcycle Game, I know how much you two like to race each other. [Ring Ring] I guess he must be busy, I'll just leave him a naughty little voicemail and maybe he'll call back quicker.

OWEN:

All done mommy…. I'm ready to go back and play now!

TORRI:

Ok, wash your hands little man and let's go. As soon as we opened the bathroom door to leave out, he took off like a speeding bullet to those arcade games [laugh] Sorry ladies I didn't think I would be in there so long with him, so anyway what was the last thing we were talking about [as I sit back in my seat]

EVA:

I don't know girl [giggle] Me and Amanda were getting to know each other, and we ordered another round of drinks while you were gone. We even got Owen a soda, just in case he gets thirsty from all that running around he's been doing.

AMANDA:

Well actually Eva….. Me and Torri was playing a little footsy under the table before you got here. I'm not wearing any panties under my jean skirt, and I was just about to see if her skirt was panty-less as well then you interrupted us [laughing]!!

EVA:

Oh Shit……now you guys are playing a game I like! Well if she's not, then that would make 3 of us, because I'm not wearing any panties under my Red Skirt either!

NARARTOR:

At this point everybody shoes are off under the table, and thank god for the long table cloth, because its 3-pair of legs wide open underneath craving pedicured toes in there wet thirsty pussy's as we speak. All their seats are pushed all the way up to the table, and nobody knows who foot is between whose legs right now. Eva's head is the first to rock back in her seat, eyes closed and damn near licking the lipstick off of her top lip. Then Torri's head is next, biting her bottom lip so seductively you can tell someone has a big toe inside her. Lastly Amanda closed her eyes just the same, and by the way she's gripping her wine glass, there's definitely a smooth foot going right up her fur box nice and slowly. From the top of the table in the public eye everything seems like normal, just 3-Ladies having drinks laughing and catching up on old times. But down yonder, 3-Women's Feet are getting more pussy than your average gigolo on a generous night. Each of these women nails are gripping the table cloth so tight, its wrinkling the whole design the "Big Arcade Place" was trying to display for the public.

TORRI:

Oh yes ladies, use those toes on this soaking wet pussy I got over here, I don't know which one of your toes this is, but yall better be glad my son is here cause I definitely would have crawled under this table smelling both of your feet to see which one of you just had your foot inside of me. Please believe I know my scent [laughing]

EVA:

[Laughing loudly] Girl you are too funny, you almost made me spit out this drink! Come on Torri, grab your glass….. let's make a toast to "New Friendships". I really like you Amanda, I think we're all going to be really good friends. (Cheers)

AMANDA:

Same here Eva, you really seem cool.

TORRI:

I feel the same way ladies, let's drink up. [Drinking wine]

EVA:

We can't forget about Owen's soda that I ordered; Amanda tell him to come drink some of his soda real quick.

AMANDA:

Oh right right [deviously] I'll take it to him. First I have to find my shoes shit, it's like 6-Loose shoes under this damn table. [laughing]

TORRI:

I know girl, with our freaky asses! So…. while Amanda's over there with Owen, what do you think of Amanda Miss Lady in Red?

EVA:

I think she's very sexy, and those tits are amazing. I can't believe she can fit all of them under that tank top [laughs]

TORRI:

I know right….. Awwwww man Eva, I think I might have drunk too much wine, I don't feel too good.

EVA:

You probably just need some fresh air, let's go outside in the parking lot and chill by your car.

AMANDA:

What's wrong Torri, you look sick. Owen didn't want much of his soda so I'll save it for him, maybe he can drink more of it later.

TORRI:

Me and Eva are about to step outside for some fresh air, you coming with us?

AMANDA:

Sure I'll cum [giggles] I mean come!

TORRI:

Ok, I can't leave Owen in here by himself though. Let me go over there and ask Mr. Baxter if he'll keep an eye on Owen while we're outside. I walk over to where Mr. Baxter is sitting and ask very kindly, even though our last encounter at home depot was very brutal. How you doing Mr. Baxter.....

MR. BAXTER:

Hello Torri, fancy meeting you here!

TORRI:

I was just wondering if you could keep an eye on Owen, while I step outside real quick. I been drinking some wine, and I'm starting to feel dizzy.

MR. BAXTER:

I'm sorry.... I just called my wife and told her I'm about to come home and eat real fast, because I have to be back up here in a hour for My Team's Tournament.

TORRI:

Oh alright I understand.

NARARATOR:

And at that exact moment a couple teenagers walk right between Torri and Mr. Baxter while they were in mid-conversation [very rudely] gossiping and giggling; "Excuse us old man"!!

TORRI:

What did they just say?

MR. BAXTER:

Just let it go Torri…. this is there arcade play place, I don't fit in up here with these young kids. I just came to bowl that's it. They weren't lying though, I am an old man.

TORRI:

That's right you came to Bowl, not to be disrespected! Excuse me little girls…. [Clears throat] I said….. EXCUSE ME Little Girls!! They turn around slowly……You young ladies need to come back over here and apologize to My Uncle and Me. First you walked right through us while we were having a conversation, and then you offended him with rude comments about his age. [Girls] "We don't have to do anything, you're not our parents". I reply….." I don't have to be your Parents, I come here all the time with my son, so I definitely recognize YOU (Pizza Girl)! I would love to tell your manager how much pot you smoke in the alley while you're on your lunch break. [Girls] I don't know what pot you're talking about….. but I'm sorry for bumping you "Mr. Uncle" and you actually don't look that old at all, got to go see you!

MR. BAXTER:

Why thank you Torri, I guess you're not so bad after all. I still don't know how you knew that girl was smoking pot, but whatever you did it worked.

TORRI:

You said it best at home depot….. I'm a Sneaky Bitch!! [Laughing]….. Well, let me go outside with my friends I have them waiting on me over there, don't worry about that favor either, I'll just take Owen outside with me. See you later Uncle Baxter [giggling]

MR. BAXTER:

Alright Niece! [Giggling]

EVA:

About time girl, let's go outside!!

TORRI:

We get outside and that air feels so good, I lean on my car cause if felt like the whole world was spinning super fast.

OWEN:

Mommy I don't feel good, I'm dizzy.

TORRI:

Me too baby…. Hey Amanda & Eva, do you guys feel dizzy as well?

EVA:

Nope, and there's a reason why we don't!

TORRI:

[Feeling drugged] And why is that? What the fuck is going on, my tongue feels numb. Owen are you ok baby? Owen….. Owen…… Owen, what the fuck have you bitches done to my son?

AMANDA:

I'm so sorry Torri…..

TORRI:

Sorry for what? Where the fuck is Owen?

AMANDA:

He's laid out in the backseat of your car.

EVA:

Fuck all that explaining shit…. We "Date Raped" You and your Son bitch! By the time you wake up, we'll be in the "Airports Parking Garage" waiting on your beloved husband to come save the day.

TORRI:

My husssssband issssssssssss going to kill youuuuuuu bitc……….!

EVA:

Yeah I'm betting on it….. "Sweet Dreams Mrs. Castle"! [Snickering] Come on Amanda, help me put her in the backseat too.

AMANDA:

You didn't give Owen that much right? His little immune system won't be able to tolerate a higher dosage.

EVA:

Shut the fuck up Mandy!! I'm the Doctor remember, he's no good to me dead anyhow stop being a dumb-ass. Now get in the driver seat and take us over to the Airport, I'll call Julius from Torri's phone. [Dialing Julius]

JULIUS:

[Phone ringing] Hello Torri…. thank God you called! I just got your voicemail and I'm on my way up there to the "Big Arcade Place" right now. If you're around Amanda, listen to me baby……. [Whispering] Don't trust her she has an Older Sister that just so happen to be My Therapist this whole time.

EVA:

Hi Julius…. Oh I'm sorry are you looking for Torri? She's a little occupied at the moment, but maybe you want to speak to Owen? Oh sorry…. he's a little occupied at the moment also [Laughing]

JULIUS:

Dr. Robinson I beg you, please leave my family out of this! I'll do whatever you need me to do just don't hurt them.

EVA:

I'm not going to hurt them Julius, I gave them a date rape drug, so if I were to kill them now, they actually won't feel a thing.

JULIUS:

Please don't do that [crying] What do you want from me?

EVA:

Meet me at the "Airport Self-Parking Garage Level 4 Section D". And I already read your Police Protocol Book also....... Me and Amanda haven't broken any laws so I don't think you'll be bringing any type of back up with you [laughing]. Your Families waiting.......[hangs up phone]

JULIUS:

Shit shit shit!! Ok ok ok Level 4 Section D. Let me call Captain so he can at least be in the loop just in case something happens to me. [Dialing Captain]

CAPTAIN:

Julius..... what the fuck is going on, did you ever find out anymore information on these crazy bitches that's trying to set you up?

JULIUS:

Can't really talk Capt. I'm speeding through traffic, meet me at the Airport Self-Parking Garage Level 4 Section D in about 20-minutes. [Hangs up]

CAPTAIN:

Parking garage level what? Fuck he hung up!

JULIUS:

I finally get there and see Dr. Robinson & Amanda standing by Torri's car. I hop out my car quick as a cat….. Where is Torri? Where is Owen? What the fuck have you two done with them.

AMANDA:

They're laid out in the backseat, Torri's moving around….. Hey Eva I think Torri's starting to wake up.

EVA:

Well wake that bitch up then Mandy!

AMANDA:

Come on Torri, let me help you out the car, Julius is here.

NARARATOR:

Torri staggers when she gets out the car, her vision is blurry from the side-effects of the drug but still manages to stand her ground. Then Eva pulls out a pistol, walks over to Torri, slaps the shit out of her in the face, then grabs a fist full of hair from the back of her neck, and places the barrel of the gun at the temple of Torri's head saying.......

EVA:

Tell your husband how I fucked you the other day with a 11-inch Dildo in a strangers house! Tell him how you ate my pussy & ass at the gym inside of a dressing room, and that's why you were late picking up your Son!! [whispering in her ear] Tell'em Bitch..... Tell'em you're a cunt eating bitch that loves pussy more than he does!!!

JULIUS:

What is she talking about Torri, is all of this true?

TORRI:

Yes Julius, but you already know how I feel about women, so please don't be mad. I told you my pussy has your name on it, I never cheated on you with a Man ever.

EVA:

Yeah yeah blah blah blah.... Throw you're Gun & Badge over to me, or I'm going to shoot your wife.

JULIUS:

Ok ok, just stay calm and I'll do whatever you say. Here's my gun....... and honestly I don't have my badge.

EVA:

Where the fuck is it?

JULIUS:

I swear I don't know, I think I left it at the precinct after running out so fast.

AMANDA:

Fuck the badge Eva, Owen's still not waking up! I think you gave him too much drugs in that soda. Is it still in the cup-holder in the car, I need to smell how strong it is.

TORRI:

Please Eva…. let me check on my son, I'm his mother please!

EVA:

Oh….. now you're his Mommy. But you pay my Little Sister to watch him for you, and you neglect him for pussy! What kind of Mommy are you then Torri? [Sticking the gun in her mouth] Don't act like you can't handle this gun, you had a 11-inch cock in your mouth the other day slut.

JULIUS:

Stop this Dr. Robinson……what are we doing in this Airport Garage, what are we doing period? You have both guns, just let Torri & Owen go, than we can handle whatever it is we need to handle.

AMANDA:

Alright everybody, Owen's breathing normal, he's doing a little tossing & turning in the backseat. He should be waking up soon.

NARARATOR:

Eva takes the gun out of Torri's mouth and pushes her down to the ground.

EVA:

Well..... let's get this show on the road then; Even I have some dignity for myself not to let children watch porn, so let's hurry up before he wakes up fully.

JULIUS:

What porn? Are you fucking nuts bitch?

EVA:

Nope, but I'm about to be full of some! Take this other gun Mandy, I want you to pick up Torri off the ground, and remove all of her clothes now! Julius pull down your pants right now as well! Bring her over here Amanda......Get up on the hood of this car Torri I want to show you something.

NARARATOR:

Torri climbed her naked body on top of that cold car's hood crying and whimpering her entire climb. As soon as she got settled up there, Eva shoved the pistol right up her pussy and said.......

EVA:

Don't move bitch, this is a stick up [laughing]

TORRI:

OUCH OUCH OUCH!!! [Painful gestures]

NARARATOR:

Torri's mouth was wide open but unable to cry, her eyes rolled in the back of her head while tears ran down her cheeks from the pain of that gun rammed up her baby maker. Julius just stared in amazement, and a tear rolled down his face too.

EVA:

As I make your Husband undress me in front of you, I want to know if you recognize this Lingerie Piece I'm wearing. Hurry up Julius….. take this red skirt off of me! I'll give you a hint Torri, its "Pink & Crotchless" [giggles]

JULIUS:

Eva….. can you at least take the gun from out of my wife, you have us all out here naked in a Parking Garage. I apologize for killing your Father and Brother, I'm so sorry; [crying] I wish I could take it back but I can't. Please don't kill my family.

EVA:

Listen Torri….. I'm about to make your husband fuck me in your face girl [giggles], and just know that I'm going to keep this pistol in your pussy the entire time, so that each back-shot thrust he gives me, I'm going to shove this gun further up inside you!! And if he doesn't cum inside of me like I want him too, then I'm going to pull this trigger, and that means "No More Babies For You"! Come here Daddy Castle stick that dick inside Dr. Robinson

NARARATOR:

Julius looks at his wife with a look of defeat, she's naked on top of the hood of the car, Eva's bending over with her ass in the air for the taking, while still having that gun inside Torri, and Amanda's just looking on while holding the other gun. Julius rubs his limp cock up and down Eva's ass crack until it eventually gets hard for insertion. Julius spread Eva's ass cheeks open and slid his dick right inside of her.......

EVA:

OOOOOOOH YES!! Now that's what I been missing..... Don't cry Mrs. Castle [talking while having sex] "Ooooooh" look at it this way "ahhhhh ahhhh ooooh, damn Julius you got a big dick ahhhhh" look at it this way...... 9-months from now Owen will have a Sister or a Brother to play with "oooooooh fuck, damn this shit is good" "Go faster Go faster..... ooooooh ooooooh you gone make me cum"

NARARATOR:

Julius pounded Eva from the back hard as he could, and fast as he could trying to hurry up and cum quick, and every time he did that the gun shoved poor little Torri's vagina until she actually started liking it. As she watched Julius fuck the shit out of Eva, her penetrations from the pistol started becoming enjoyable. Torri started grabbing her tits playing with her own nipples, and eventually she yelled out..... "Ooooooooh Fuck her Julius, Fuck her Julius, Fuck that Crazy Bitch I'm about to cum on this pistol….. Oh Shit Yea Yea"!!! Pinching her nipples harder & harder I'MMMMM CUMMMMING!!

EVA:

ME TOO!!! FUCK ME FUCK ME FUCK ME……OOOOOOOH I'M CUMMMIN TOO!!!!

JULIUS:

OH SHIT….. I'M 'BOUT TO CUM! OHHHHHHH HOLY SHIT I'M CUMMMMMMIN TOO!!!

NARARTOR:

Eva pulls the gun out of Torri very exhaustedly; See Torri, the point was to never kill any of you, the whole idea was to destroy Julius's life, because he destroyed ours. Now I'll be carrying his baby, and my crazy ass will be a part of your family for the rest of our lives [Laughs devilishly]. Julius pulls his sperm leaking dick out of Eva, grabs the gun out of her hand and pushes her to the ground.

JULIUS:

Hurry up honey get in the car with Owen! Hurry hurry pull off pull off!!

TORRI:

Shoot that cunt bitch Julius!

AMANDA:

Drop the gun Mr. Castle and let my sister stand up.

EVA:

[Laughing] That's right Mandy, it's about time you got some balls!

AMANDA:

Shut the fuck up Eva, I'm so sick of you telling me what to do.

EVA:

What are you talking about?

AMANDA:

I'm talking about you Eva......I almost succeeded in getting rid of you out my life a long time ago, but it didn't work. This time I'm going to make sure the job gets done!

EVA:

A long time ago, what the fuck are you talking about?

AMANDA:

Mom wasn't supposed to drink (Your) cup of tea that morning, once she burned her tongue, you switched the cups, and fucked everything up! You we're supposed to die that day not Mom, I specifically made that poison for you, and now she's gone and your still here [crying]! But I won't have that problem anymore [aiming the gun at Eva]

117

EVA:

NO MANDY!! DON'T SHOOT ME!!!

CAPTAIN:

Freeze Police…. Put that gun down Missy or I swear to god I'll shoot your ass.

JULIUS:

Cap…. you showed up just in time, there's another gun over there by Dr. Robinson.

CAPTAIN:

Why the fuck is everybody naked? Don't you move a muscle babysitter I still got my eye on you.

JULIUS:

It's a long story Captain, I'll tell you all about it over a cup of coffee one day.

AMANDA:

I know what your thinking Eva…. don't even think about grabbing that gun.

EVA:

We supposed to be Sister's, were supposed to be Blood, and you have the nerve to want me dead bitch [Eva goes for the gun]

CAPTAIN:

Freeze Dr. Robinson! Don't Do It, I said.... Don't Do It!!

AMANDA:

NO............

NARARATOR:

Amanda jumps in front of Eva, and The Captain fires off 2-shots from his 9-milimeter aimed straight for Eva, but Amanda's body is the one who takes all the bullets.

EVA:

NOOOOOOOOOOO!!!!

NARARATOR:

Eva catches Amanda's body before it even hits the ground. [Hollering] No God No No No! Amanda looks eye to eye with Eva and says.....

AMANDA:

Everything is alright sister, I Love You.

EVA:

I Love You too sister.

AMANDA:

Tell Owen that I Love Him, and tell Torri I never meant for any harm to come to him.

EVA:

Ok Mandy, I Love You, just hold on until the ambulance gets here. You're not going to die, I'm the one that deserves to die [crying]

AMANDA:

Eva….. Eva…. I can see Mom. She's just as beautiful as we remembered her [smiling] Bye Eva see you soon…….

CAPTAIN:

Don't move Dr. Robinson your under arrest!

NARARATOR:

The Captain threw the hand-cuffs on Eva while she sat there in shock over her dead sister. Julius & Torri put their clothes on and was fully dressed by the time the rest of the Police Department showed up to the scene. Owen had a little headache from the soda, but he was ok all an all. The ambulance showed up and gave everyone blankets and water, and still did a minor check on all of the survivor's that was still at the Airport Garage.

JULIUS:

Come on everyone, let's go home. I Love You Torri! Daddy Loves You Owen!!

TORRI:

I Love You too!

OWEN:

I Love You too Daddy, I'm hungry!!

JULIUS:

Me too son, go ahead and get in the car Owen, we're about to get ready and leave. Me and your Mom just have to thank the Captain again.

CAPTAIN:

Go ahead and get out of her Castle….. we're going to impound your wife's car overnight because it may have evidence on it. Get your family in order, and then I'll see you at the precinct tomorrow morning.

OWEN:

Oooooh Daddy left a DVD on the seat. I bet it's a cartoon from the video store [smiling] It must be a surprise for me yay……. I'll just put it in my pocket, and then play it once we get home on the big TV.

JULIUS:

Alright Captain, I'll see you tomorrow. Let me open that passenger door for you honey.

TORRI:

Thank you babe….. we drive off in Julius's car all 3 of us in the front seat bundled up in our ambulance blankets. I can't wait to get home and lay in my bed Julius, I need a long hot bath and some clean sheets. We finally pull up to the house and all I can think of was "Home Sweet Home"! We jumped out of the car, unlock our front door, and we all just fell inside the living room. I immediately ran me and Julius some warm bath water with bubbles just how we both like it. Owen disappeared in his room somewhere, but Me & Julius focused on our own alone time. After about 10-minutes the tub was ready, Julius gets in first, and then I sit in front of him between his legs and just lay the back of my head on his chest relaxed & relieved that all this shit was over. I blurt out…." I am so so so sorry about all the sneaking around I did with Eva, I really became obsessed with the whole Lesbian experience and didn't realize what I was doing.

JULIUS:

Don't worry about it boo, let's try to put this night behind us and tomorrow is a new day.

TORRI:

Your right…... I'm just so glad that you never fucked around with Eva or should I say Dr. Robinson (besides tonight)! You didn't let her beauty seduce you, and you stayed loyal to our marriage, I Love your strength. But I will say this……I don't know what protocol method you Police Officers use when it comes to pregnant women in jail, but if that bitch gets pregnant with your baby, I'll rob a store on purpose just to get locked up, and then beat a miscarriage out that hoe! [Laughing] But it was weird that you didn't have your Badge, that's not like you baby, you always have it.

JULIUS:

I know, but I was rushing to save you guys and I think I left it at the precinct.

TORRI:

Rushing to save us….. Awwww my SuperMan!! I still can't believe Amanda is dead, she was such a sweet girl, but in a psychopath sort of way. [Laughing]

JULIUS:

Yea they really we're messed up in the head…. what is that noise? That sounds like Owen in the Living Room, what is he doing now?

TORRI:

Let me go check, I'll be right back sweetie. [dripping water out the tub] Owen what are you doing in here darling? And who showed you how to load the DVD Player?

OWEN:

Amanda showed me last time she baby-sitted me.

TORRI:

Oh really [smiling] and what are you about to watch?

OWEN:

I don't know….. some DVD that was in Daddy's car earlier, I hope it's a good cartoon.

JULIUS:

So what is he doing in there Torri?

TORRI:

He's trying to watch a DVD he got out your car earlier.

JULIUS:

DVD in my car? (Hmmmmm), I didn't have any dvd's…. OH FUCK THE PORNO!!! [jumping out the tub] Take it out Torri, hurry up and take it out, don't let him see it.

TORRI:

What's wrong Julius…. it's just a work-out video on how to lose weight. Why did you jump out the tub like that?

JULIUS:

Oh, I thought it was a Surveillance Video of this murder I'm investigating. I didn't want Owen to have any nightmares that's all. I go back in the bathroom by myself and close the door……(what the fuck) if that's not the DVD with Me & Eva on it….. then where is it?

NARARATOR:

Meanwhile at the "Big Arcade Place"..... Mr. Baxter and his twin brother we're winning a championship trophy for the best players in the Tournament. They took pictures and popped champagne. After about 20-minutes went by Mr. Baxter was ready to hop in his old school Cadillac and rush home to his wife to spread the glory. Once he made it home, he parked in the driveway and got out his vehicle with the most confidence. A shiny glare shot off the grass from the reflection of the porch light. Mr. Baxter walked closer to it, and reached down in the grass. It was a Policeman's badge, and he was thinking how weird that was. There was only one Cop in their neighborhood, so it must belong to Julius, but what would his badge be doing in their yard? Mr. Baxter put it in his pocket and strolled in the house. Once inside he yelled...... "Honey your Champion is Home"!! He gets in the living room and see's Mrs. Baxter laid on the couch half naked in a silk gown sleep.

MR. BAXTER:

Honey..... what are you doing? And what is that smell?

MRS. BAXTER:

[Yawning and stretching] Oh hey honey, I thought you were coming home earlier to eat? You made me warm up that food for nothing. I tried to wait up for you, but I guess I feel asleep.

MR. BAXTER:

Yeah..... I decided to stay up there with Twin because he didn't want to miss our turn. Why are you half naked on the couch dressed in that short ass gown, and why does it smell like sex in here?

MRS. BAXTER:

Well if you must know......I was trying to surprise you with this Lingerie Gown when you got home, but you took so long I masturbated and fell asleep.

MR. BAXTER:

You know we don't have anymore condoms left in the drawer, so how were you going to surprise me?

MRS. BAXTER:

Nevermind nevermind….. you always know how to mess up a mood! I'm going to bed (Goodnight)

NARARATOR:

Soon as Mrs. Baxter got off the couch, a DVD was in between the crevices and some kind of milky substance stuck on it. He made sure Mrs. Baxter was all the way upstairs before he put the DVD in. [Remote clicks play] He saw Julius inside some kind of business office getting his dick sucked by a beautiful Business Woman, and now it started making sense.

MR. BAXTER:

So my wife is masturbating or hiding a DVD of Julius having sex huh, and not to mention I find his Badge in my grass……. I hope what I think is going on isn't going on, but I'm not going to jump to conclusions until I know for sure. I pull the DVD out of the Player and start walking over to the Castle's house, Badge in one hand and DVD in the other. [Ring Doorbell]

NARARATOR:

[Ding Dong] At this moment, Torri and Julius are back in the tub kissing & touching, and being very grateful for one another, especially after the night they just had.

JULIUS:

Now what? Just when we're comfortable in a warm tub, somebody ringing the damn doorbell.

TORRI:

Go ahead and answer it babe, I'm about to go in our bedroom and lotion up. My pussy stills hurt from that gun being rammed up there, but I'm so proud of you, I'm going to let you fuck me in my ass tonight! Now hurry up and answer the door and get back in here Mr. Castle.

JULIUS:

You better stopped playing with me, you never let me fuck you in the ass. Let me grab my robe and get rid of this character at the door. I walked barefoot to the door, and turn on the porch light. I look through the peek hole and it's Mr. Baxter. I open the door and greet him "Hey Mr. Baxter what you doing out this late"?

MR. BAXTER:

I came over to drop some of your belongings off to you I had in my possession.

JULIUS:

Possessions? What would you have of mine?

MR. BAXTER:

Well for starter's your Badge was in my grass.... not sure how that got in there but here you go Officer.

JULIUS:

I've told Owen a million times to stop playing with my badge. I appreciate you returning it to me Mr. Baxter.

MR. BAXTER:

No problem..... And one more thing I know you really need.

JULIUS:

Oh, and what is that?

MR. BAXTER:

This DVD my wife seemed to be hiding for you. I watched some of it..... The Women in the All White looks just like Torri I must say. [Sarcasticly laughs]

JULIUS:

I quickly step onto the porch with Mr. Baxter in my robe and close the door gently. Look this DVD was a mistake and you have to promise not to mention this to Torri ok Mr. Baxter?

MR. BAXTER:

Listen up Fuck Stick......you should be ashamed of yourself cheating on that gorgeous woman you got in there. I had a lot of respect for you Mr. Castle, but after today you can go to hell!

JULIUS:

Easy for you to say "Old Man"......some of us men actually get erections all day every day. It's not my fault your dick doesn't get hard no more. [Laughs]

MR. BAXTER:

What are you talking about?

JULIUS:

Mrs. Baxter told me all about your little limp dick problem [giggles]

MR. BAXTER:

Oh really, well I hope for your sake you didn't do anything with my wife because that would be very bad for you Sir..... [Balling up his fist]

JULIUS:

Mr. Baxter please..... what the fuck you gone do to me! I just witnessed my Babysitter die in front of my eyes, and did things tonight so dangerous You & Your Wife's drama couldn't even compare. I'm a motherfucking Police Officer, so yeah I fucked your Wife to keep my name good with my family. She was blackmailing me so I did it (what the fuck you going to do)!!

MR. BAXTER:

I guess you really enjoy living on the edge huh Mr. Castle?

JULIUS:

Maybe, why you say that?

MR. BAXTER:

Listen….. You don't have to worry about me saying anything to your Wife about this Video alright.

JULIUS:

Alright then…. now that's more like it!

MR. BAXTER:

I will never have to tell her anything, because eventually you'll tell on yourself.

JULIUS:

And why would I do something like that?

MR. BAXTER:

Because…….. My Wife has had HIV for the last 10-years! It's not that my dick that won't get hard to fuck her [giggles] It's the fact that she hates condoms. She craves Raw Sex, but we can't chance it cause of The Virus! Now….. was your night still more dangerous then Me and My Wife's little bullshit Drama?

JULIUS:

WAIT……….. WAIT……….… ARE YOU FUCKING SERIOUS!!!

TORRI:

Come on Big Daddy..…. I'm waiting on you JULIUS!!!

MR. BAXTER:

WELL GO AHEAD MR. CASTLE……. SEEMS LIKE YOUR WIFE IS CALLING YOU! [Whistling off the porch].

THE END

Printed in the United States
By Bookmasters